NEW MAPS

deindustrial fiction

VOL. 3, NO. 3
SUMMER 2023

LOOSELEAF PUBLISHING

Bayfield, Wisconsin

About New Maps

New Maps publishes stories in the growing genre of deindustrial fiction, which explores the long decline of industrial civilization, its aftermath, and the new worlds made possible by its departure. The magazine also publishes essays, book reviews, letters to the editor, and other content that examines these themes. For more on the philosophy of the magazine, see the website below, or get acquainted by way of this issue.

Submissions of any of the foregoing may be addressed to the editor at either of the addresses below. Story submission guidelines may be found on the website or requested by post.

New Maps is published quarterly by Looseleaf Publishing. Subscriptions are currently available in the U.S., Australia, Belgium, Canada, Germany, Hong Kong, Ireland, Japan, the Netherlands, New Zealand, Sweden, Taiwan, and the U.K. An annual subscription is $48.00 USD for U.S. addresses, with different prices elsewhere, and may be purchased from the website below, or by writing to request an order form.

Postal correspondence:	Online:
Looseleaf Publishing	www.new-maps.com
87095 Valley Road	editor@new-maps.com
Bayfield, WI 54814, USA	

ISSN: 2767-388X

Copyright © August 2023 by Looseleaf Publishing. All stories and essays in this magazine are copyrighted by their respective authors and used here with permission. All rights reserved.

Image credits:
- Cover art: *Factory Ruin on the Battenkill, Rexleigh, New York,* by James Howard Kunstler, copyright 2015.
- Music on p. 57 copyright 2023 by Wesley Stine.

The stories contained herein are works of fiction. All characters and events portrayed in the stories in this publication are fictional, and any semblance to real people or events is purely coincidental.

Contents

Introduction iv
Letters 1

Essays & Sundries   9
Cheap Thrills: Radio's Next Golden Age 11

WB Rice
And There Was 20

Stories   23

Clint Spivey
Rocketsonde 25

Wesley Stine
Luna the Kitten 42

Cal Bannerman
Lights Out 60

Anthony St. George
Navigating the Immortals 66

R. Jean Mathieu
Glâcehouse 81

About This Issue   102
Contributors 102
Colophon & Acknowledgments 104

Introduction

Something I've thought about a few times is whether there's any chance that the "end of the world" might soon settle itself on us so fully that *New Maps* becomes obsolete: that is, that we will already be in the deindustrial future, and "deindustrial fiction" will just be another name for "contemporary fiction." Fortunately, I don't think there is: it seems likely that, for as long as my lifetime lasts at least, wherever we find ourselves in the decline, there will always be waypoints further down the trail. A decline and fall take a while, and though this one's been underway for some time already, it also has quite a ways to go.

But each new ratcheting-down can feel like a fresh new apocalypse. Because I'm releasing this issue so late in the summer—it's August as I write—I can comment that this summer has felt more apocalyptic than a number of previous ones. I think after COVID ended (to the extent it actually "ended," something I'm not prepared to comment on with any semblance of authority), a lot of us thought we'd go back to 2019, or maybe, if we were *really* feeling done with the plague time, back to 1999. Last year, where I live anyway, the hard truth was still easy enough to ignore that I could pretend we'd managed the trick.

But this year, well. Globally: heat records, global realignment, inflation. Locally: ash-reddened skies from Canadian fires, a plague of mosquitoes (the old-timers say it's the worst they've seen), a plague of spongy moths denuding whole hillsides of oaks.

It's a bracing time to be alive. And catastrophe hasn't even hit me specifically, so far.

But what to do? Keep collapsing and try to stay ahead of the rush—the yurt that I've been working on is made with hand tools and a sawmill that's on the build site, and my new secondhand bicycle trailer is one of (19-month-old) Ivor's favorite ways to get around. In fact, aside from dread about the sky and the oaks, I've had a good summer, and I've spent most of it barefoot and outside.

And keep telling stories. Stories about your own life, stories about your children's and inheritors' lives, stories about the future of nature and of humanity. Stories to believe that the future just might have a place for us after all. Here are five stories that deal with technologies new and old. They take us in wildly different directions; in the Letters section, I hail the way of "dissensus" as a helpful if chaotic path forward, and here are stories of all sorts of futures. Enjoy, and welcome to the strange new world we're constantly entering.

—Nathanael Bonnell
Editor

Letters

New Maps *welcomes letters, whether to the editor or as part of a conversation between readers in the Letters section. Email* editor@new-maps.com, *with "Letter" somewhere in the subject line, and sign with your name as you'd like it to be printed. Or write via post, including your name and a note to consider your letter for publication, to Looseleaf Publishing, 87095 Valley Rd., Bayfield, WI 54814, U.S.A.*

Readers,

The first several letters this month pertain to Wesley Stine's letter in the previous issue, in which he proposed the idea of a periodical "awards issue" for New Maps. *For more detail on Stine's idea, refer back to the previous issue. —NB*

☉

Hey Nathanael,

I love the idea of awards for the deindustrial fiction genre.

In the early-ish days of *Astounding* magazine, they used to publish, monthly, a ranking of stories from a previous issue. People would write in (by letter, of course) and rank the stories, and the rankings would be averaged, so that a story that was voted top by everyone would get a score of 1.0. The stories for that issue would then be ranked. They later changed it to an annual thing with a voting form, categories, etc., but the chaos of that early system still really appeals to me. It was noticeable, for example, that longer stories almost always did better than shorter ones, and you can't tell this any more as they are voted for separately.

Anyway, just a thought: I love the idea of readers voting for their favorite stories in each issue. And then there could be an annual awards thing as well.

BTW: I definitely agree with you that the readers, not the writers, should be the ones voting/nominating.

Whatever you end up with, I'll be excited to see it and hopefully participate in it.

Cheers!
Ben Coppin

Dear Nathanael, Wesley, and fellow *New Maps* readers and writers,

It was with great excitement that I read Wesley Stine's letter to the editor, and his idea of a having awards for *New Maps* authors. I have mixed feelings about this notion, but I was still excited by his letter, as it got me thinking about fandom and the potential for a subculture to grow around deindustrial fiction, and what we as the individual and collective seedbearers of such a culture might do to help it germinate.

Deindustrial fiction is a problem child of science fiction. We share a common ancestry that links our work to Mary Shelley's. In the same way Shelley wrestled with the monstrous creations of science, we wrestle with the world in the aftermath of a scientific age, the downslope of progress. We also deal with the many futures to be encountered on Earth—and SF has long dealt with "the future." That's what makes us a problem child: the futures we depict don't conform to the now-standard SF boilerplate of "the future."

Frankenstein was published in 1818. Jules Verne, Edgar Allan Poe, and Robert Louis Stevenson continued the trend and all started writing early SF material as the 1800s clattered on. H. G. Wells added his imaginative flourishes to the form in the 1890s. As the 1900s got underway more writers tried their hand at it, and its popularity really picked up with the coming of SF pulps, riding on the back of the penny dreadful. *Amazing Stories* put out its first issue in 1926. SF started to proliferate. The first World Science Fiction Convention, or Worldcon, was held in 1939. The convention itself was put together by the World Science Fiction Society (WSFS), a group whose sole aim, at least in the early years, was to promote SF. They didn't award a writer with the first Hugo until the eleventh Worldcon in 1953, and Alfred Bester was the winner with his still fantastic novel *The Demolished Man*. I've read it, and a lot of older SF fans have read it, but I'm not sure how well read it is beyond those who have a deep affinity for SF. The Nebula award wasn't established until thirteen years later in 1966 and is given by the Science Fiction and Fantasy Writers Association, modeled on the Edgar, given by the Mystery Writers of America. One of the commonalities of these organizations is that they are not tied to a single publisher or magazine, but can pick the person awarded from within a field and ecosystem of publishing.

Deindustrial fiction doesn't have that ecosystem yet, but it doesn't mean we can't.

As active retrovators we can look to the past for inspiration and look and see what others did to promote the literature they loved. SF has the WSFS. An interested party could take it upon themselves to start a deindustrial fiction society and begin the work of getting more ink spilled about endeavors in this vein. It was the WSFS who put together the first Worldcon after smaller get-togethers had been started. A society that had yearly dues, elbow grease and gumption could put a deindustrial con together in time (hopefully at a convenient city within the Midwest).

Yet transportation, timing and economics always leave some fans and authors out of attending a convention. As our society goes through its various stages of unravelment, this will probably be continue to make it difficult, but not impossible. These people could still participate in another grand SF tradition that helped spread of the genre: zines. Just like its latter-day punk rock counterpart, the SF zine was the place where fans brought their amateur stories, reflections, and critically, their reviews of SF literature. This was the roundtable place where the geeks gathered to talk about the literature. A 'zine is a good place to praise, debate, or lambaste a story, while also rounding up any news and announcements from within the subculture.

In the underground music world, zines were the primary way of exchanging information. Punk, industrial, and gothic music didn't get the same kind of press coverage as bands on major labels. Yet indie music thrived, and without any kind of official awards. The peacenik anarcho-punk band Crass were a living expression of this DIY ethos. Their first album *The Feeding of the 5000* was self-recorded, self-released, self-promoted. The first pressing sold out immediately. They sold enough copies of the album for it to go gold, and then platinum. Their albums have remained in print since that first one came out in 1978, reissued in a number of formats and editions, and recently remastered. Yet at Dial House where Crass members Penny Rimbaud and Gee Vaucher still live, you won't see an official platinum record hanging on the wall. That's because they've never been associated with the record industry people who keep track of major label sales and give out awards. Crass left their mark all the same and continue to draw in new fans.

There are so many great independent music acts who will never receive a Grammy despite their legions of devoted fans within a self-supporting and self-sustaining subculture. Fans who would let the band crash and party at their punk house so they didn't have to fork over dough for a motel, fans who would write up reviews and advocate about their favorite albums in a slew of different zines, fans who promoted the thing they loved and shared it with their friends and family. The same was true of the SF subculture in its early years.

I remember in junior high when I received a mixtape from a punker a few years older than me who had moved in down the street. The sounds of the Descendants, the Ramones, Minor Threat, Black Flag, Sex Pistols and Crass opened up my mind to another musical reality. After I saw my first fanzine I knew I wanted to make my own. Getting the word about the deindustrial genre could literally open up a door for someone and change their entire life for the better.

So rather than focusing on awards, I think the readers and writers for *New Maps* (and other related venues such as Dark Mountain) should think on what we can do as individuals and collectively, to promote this area of writing to those who have yet to know it even exists.

Justin Patrick Moore
Cincinnati, Ohio

Dear Editor,
Here are my thoughts on the "awards issue" mentioned in the last issue.

First of all, I'm not a fan of contests. I used to be very excited about them, as I hoped—like any ambitious young author with an exaggerated idea of his talent—it would be just the thing to reveal my genius to the world; now, I've realized that: 1. I'm not a genius (I'm not sure they exist), and 2. You can't account for taste, and I'm often disappointed with the stories that end up winning contests (even when those stories are mine: those of my stories which ended up winning prizes/contests are those I like least).

Second, if the goal is to get feedback on the stories and start a conversation, I'm not sure a contest is the best way to do that. Contests pit stories against one another when each story should be in its own category. Feedback, of course, is always appreciated, but I'm convinced one-to-one exchanges like the ones I have with you and a few *New Maps* authors are much more productive. One of them suggested a writing workshop. (But that's perhaps complicated to organize at a distance, though video-conference is more and more common these days and maybe it wouldn't need to happen "live" but maybe on some sort of forum or something? I don't know. Perhaps this Letters section could fill that need, and it does, at times, but the three-month turnaround certainly doesn't help making it feel like a conversation, and in this the Internet might have a use.) I don't think there needs to be a contest/competition for authors (and readers, indeed) to exchange feedback. Also, I tend to think feedback made in a public forum, in front of a lot of people, is bound to be less sincere and useful than that given in one-to-one discussions.

Third, all this doesn't mean there shouldn't be a contest, just that I don't think it's the best way to get earnest feedback. Though, as I said, I'm not a fan of competition, I know others can be, and maybe an awards or anthology issue might help make the magazine more visible. If you do end up organizing one, I'm here to help. And, as you remarked in your answer to Wesley's letter, I do believe readers should vote, not just writers. I have a feeling *New Maps* (like most literary magazines, to be honest) already has a hefty share of writers in its readership anyway.

Pierre Magdelaine

Dear Ben, Justin, Pierre, and others who preferred not to be published, as well as Wesley,

Thank you all for the thought you've put in to what an "awards issue" might and might not be able to do for *New Maps*. My own thoughts about the matter were split when Wesley first broached the idea, and I can see that those thoughts mirror a split among the readership and authorship. (Readers just joining the magazine may not know that all four of the above-named letter writers have also been published here.)

One-on-one feedback on stories has always been one of the best tools for me to refine my own writing, and I've been helped by writers both involved and uninvolved with this magazine. If I had all the time in the world, I'd love to provide thoughtful, book-report-style comments on all the stories I receive, but some line-by-line comments in a Word document are usually the most I can muster while elbow-deep in the magazine-assembly process. So I'm very glad to know that some of the authors of this magazine have begun talking amongst themselves. A conversation between authors was already going as early as the Into the Ruins *days, when I was one of those authors (one of these days, I'll publish fiction in my own magazine too!), but I'm aware that it's recently picked up at least a little speed, and I should draw atten-*tion now to the comment that follows every issue's Contributors page: "Comments for contributors sent to the editor will be forwarded." Comments can be, and have been, as simple as: "Would you pass along my email address to Such-and-So? I think we could have a fruitful conversation." Readers, I should also stress, are welcome to comment whether or not they're also authors; not only writers can appreciate the craft of writing, or bookstores could never exist!

Justin's comments about building a community parallel my own wishes about publicizing *New Maps* more widely. Of course it would be modestly profitable to me if the magazine were better known, but from the start I've never been in this project for the money, or I would have given up quite a while ago. I see an anxiety about the future eating away at most people in my world, and I see, in the culture at large, mostly dysfunctional responses to that anxiety: directionless guilt that results in no personal changes is a popular one, as is an attempt to forget that there's any predicament at all. Marcu Knoesen, in the letter below, writes of the distinction between problems (which are solvable) and predicaments (which aren't). I think realizing that the end of the fossil fuel era is a predicament, not a problem, is one light-switch flip that can improve mental well-being considerably: no longer do you need to bang your head against an insoluble problem; now you can focus energy on adapting to the predicament's consequences. My first wish is for more people to flip that light switch, and my second one is that this magazine can be helpful to them in adjusting to their new worldview once they've done it.

What can help build that community? The feedback on an awards issue is one possibility. Gatherings, virtual or actual, are another. Getting the word out, getting copies of New Maps *into interested people's hands, just expanding the raw number of eyeballs that read these stories — these seem like the best first steps. Ones that, so far, I've found myself to be too few people to accomplish. Many readers have spread this magazine to their friends and family, and I'm so grateful for that. How can we spread it further and ignite the cross-pollination of ideas among members that makes a readership into a fertile ecosystem with the opportunity to grow and bloom like sci-fi or punk? If I knew the answer, I guess* New Maps *would be a lot bigger already. I have a few ideas, but yours are all very welcome.*

I don't believe I have a verdict on the possibility of an awards issue. Certainly I can't reject or accept the plan based on a unanimous vote from readers — the way of dissensus is truly and duly embraced among this readership, it seems! In the same spirit of dissensus, though — in John Michael Greer's sense of "having everyone try different things so that someone's *bound to get a good answer" — I may, one day when time permits, find it irresistible to run at least one contest: that being something I haven't done before with this magazine, and so, worthy of trying out.*

☉

I loved dinosaurs as a kid. There was just something about them. Mythical monsters that I kept being told were real but they had all just died out before humans arrived on the scene. So as a young dinosaur-obsessed boy, I was delighted when I learned that there would be a *Jurassic Park* movie with real dinosaurs on the screen. I still remember one of my second-grade classmates telling us how the movie was so gruesome that one of the audience members in an early screening went mad from the images on screen. Needless to say, I didn't get to see the movie for a few years since the PG-10 age restriction placed it squarely three years out of my reach. I went on to see the movie in excess of thirty times throughout my life. I loved the movie and later, when I discovered the book it was based on, I loved that too.

I was delighted to learn that there was a sequel in the works a few years later. At least this time I was a bit more media-savvy and could follow the news, and I was old enough to see the movie when it came out. It is the second movie in the series, *The Lost World*, that has been on my mind lately. In the movie version, there is a scene where one of the main characters, Dr. Ian Malcolm, is in a field expedition vehicle on a dinosaur-infested island with an old love interest. The love interest, Dr. Sarah Harding, has taken it upon herself to try and fix the broken leg of a baby T. rex which she brought with her to the vehicle to do an x-ray. There is a few seconds of silence in the vehicle where Ian gets to say "Hold on, this is going to be bad" just before the irate parents of the baby T. rex attack.

I can't shake the feeling that 2018 was the year we got that "Hold on, this is going to be bad" warning loud and clear. The northern hemisphere experienced crazy heat waves and out-of-control wildfires, and the Arctic experienced a raft of out-of-the-ordinary events. Maersk, the shipping company, announced their first ship passing through the Northwest Passage as the ice levels reduced enough to allow that. Here in Australia record droughts were ongoing and there had been wildfires in winter. We were warned to expect a dangerous fire season that summer. Around the same time the French environment minister resigned since he felt that there was nothing more he could do.

I learned a while ago that my father is a climate change "denier." I struggle to broach the subject with him since he doesn't really make the argument on the grounds of data and thus we have no common ground on which to argue. I understand, as far as problems go, climate change has stacked the deck. In a situation where the effects are cumulative, long-term, and mostly unpredictable, the causality is not direct and the whole situation is exacerbated simply by our way of life. So while I don't agree with my father I can understand where he is coming from, especially if one is looking for simple, clear and easy-to-understand answers.

However, one thing I feel we should all be able to agree on, climate advocates and climate deniers alike, is that if there is any uncertainty, we should err on the side of caution based on what is at stake. And yet we have a situation similar to the debate over "smoking causes cancer" where smokers just keep smoking regardless of the evidence. Perhaps until there is clarity or certainty we could try and limit the carbon dioxide emissions? Although at this stage the precautionary principle has also become a political football and I'm not sure how much more evidence the denial camp needs.

One of the themes in *Jurassic Park* was that of control, man vs. nature — the premise that man can capture nature, put a leash around it and keep it in a neat little box. The movie clearly went to show that nature won out. I fear that we may once again be playing with fire, in the Promethean sense. Most people have no idea how dependent their lives are on the biosphere, which to them is just a backdrop "out there."

There is a scene in *Jurassic Park*, the book version, where the power has gone off and the protagonists are able to turn it back on. The power outage is treated as a minor setback, and as the maintenance crews move around fixing fences and herding dinosaurs back into their paddocks, everybody thinks everything is okay. I fear this is where we are in the story.

What the people on the island don't know at this stage is that the whole park is running off the backup generator and the fuel is running low. Soon the power will go out again and then the real trouble will start.

There is a difference between problems and predicaments. Problems have solutions and predicaments you can only adapt to. I think the people in *Jurassic Park* made the mistake of confusing the two. Up until the point that it became clear that they were running on the backup generator, they thought they had a problem. The power had gone out in a storm and they just needed to fix what was damaged and get things back to normal. Meanwhile, they were actually in a predicament where the remaining normalcy was courtesy of the remaining fuel in the tank of the backup generator. If they had realized their predicament sooner they could have called in rescue helicopters while they still had communications and things might have turned out differently.

My feelings regarding climate change are the same. We had a few shudderings indicating something is amiss. A few hottest years on record, abnormal weather in the Arctic, etc. And yet we still believe we have a problem. Nothing a few wind turbines, electric cars, and a handful of yet-to-be-invented carbon-capture technologies won't fix. All the while we are actually in a predicament and even if we stopped burning fossil fuels today there would still be a reckoning.

The recent events taking place in the Northern Hemisphere have uncanny echoes of 2018. Heat records are falling like dominoes and out-of-control weather events are too numerous to keep track of. Here in Australia, we have been warned that it will likely be a very hot and dry summer.

All I can say is, hold on, this is going to be bad.

Marcu Knoesen
Australia

Dear Marcu,

Much of the world's amazingly sedate reaction to climate change can be likened to Upton Sinclair's famous maxim: "It is difficult to get a man to understand something, when his salary depends upon his not understanding it." Driving around all over the place, eating foods that a hundred years ago you'd have to travel to the tropics to find, watching color movies in a surround-sound home theater, and all the other modern things we do—why, it's all awfully fun, if you make sure not to look at its global consequences. And the alternative to having all those is—well, the alternative is what we're exploring here in this obscure corner of the cultural imagination, but popularly, there are really only a couple alternatives: a return to the Stone Age, or wholesale human extinction. And those don't bear thinking about, especially when there's another season of Game of Kardashians *coming out.*

The last few years, though, since the initial wake-up call in 2018 that you heard, have seen the alarms getting louder and more frequent. More and more people are finding it impossible to get their fingers deep enough in their ears to avoid hearing them. Some will never be reached, and to that I say that it's a good thing that a species with as much ability to change the planet as humans has at least not figured out immortality, because that allows old, maladaptive thought habits to go gradually whistling down the wind as their practitioners die, along the lines of Thomas Kuhn's description of scientific revolutions. Many will figure out they need to change their lives, though, and some of them will even do it.

That's where we'll see the precautionary principle exercised. Governments have shown that they are reliably unable to change public behavior around carbon emissions, and almost uniformly unwilling to change themselves. If anyone's going to be precautionary, it'll be us, each of us individually when we decide that's what needs to be done.

And yes, even despite that... it's gonna be bad. Reality is one helluva T. rex. —NB

☉

Instead of writing that involves magic,[1] what about writing that *is* magic? Have we forgotten the purpose of story?

It is said that we need new stories to envision our unfolding reality, ones that hold that right relationship with the rest of our living world is possible. Ones that express how we may heal from our collective traumas and embrace change, that demonstrate how we may throw over the tables of the money lenders and those casting lots on our lot. Ones that illuminate with a prescience how we may transmute the shit that we find ourselves in, like the teenagers of a burned-down South Bronx, and birth cultural revolutions as unstoppable as hip-hop, but in initiated, adult form.

We need these stories and they need us to birth them. They are inside each and every one of us. Waiting to get out. Our ancestors have written them in disappearing genetic ink that departs the moment we stop writing. We have never read them before, but they have been reading us since before we were born. So yes, let's

---

1 *See issue 3:1 (Winter 2023), the "Magic Issue"—for instance my introduction, which explains the premise for the issue. —NB*

write of magic, like Bertelsen's Ghosts in Little Deer's Grove,[2] let us weave with a spidery bendy kind of way that hollows out our egos and pulls the cords from above and below and from within and without and never loosens its grip on our souls and our soulspeech. Let it be done with ink and pen and keyboard and sounding board, and let the stories be then woven together themselves. Created as they are with the memories of all of our myriad ancestors of the ancient future unfolding before us, each a piece of the same infinite puzzle stretching out past horizon. The ugly pieces have already been revealed. It is not that we cannot shed light on the darkness, but since we are forged of it, let us look towards the light and reveal that as well so that we may be fully expressed in our wholeness.

Nathanael Secor
Washburn, Wis.

Dear fellow Nathanael,

Is not every story magic, whether it intends to be or not? I attempted to make that point in my story "The No-Account."[3] And as my character Listens Through says, "The most dangerous story of all is the one you don't know you're tellin'."

The future is poorly mapped, and I intend this magazine to show us what to seek and what to avoid, both. It's a poor navigational chart that shows all the open water and well-equipped marinas, but leaves out the shoals and the reefs and the shallow shipwrecks.

But it's also a poor sailor who beelines for Scylla, Charybdis, and the Sirens, when there are so many beautiful islands to make for. —NB

---

2 See Into the Ruins *Nos. 12–13. —NB*
3 *In* Into the Ruins *No. 11, and also available on the* New Maps *website at* www.new-maps.com/sample-work/.

ESSAYS & SUNDRIES

Radio's Next Golden Age

> *"The Ultimate Rule ought to be: 'If it sounds GOOD to you, it's bitchin'; if it sounds BAD to YOU, it's shitty.' The more your musical experience, the easier it is to define for yourself what you like and what you don't like. American radio listeners, raised on a diet of _____ (fill in the blank), have experienced a musical universe so small they cannot begin to know what they like."* —Frank Zappa, *The Real Frank Zappa Book*

Cheap Thrills
Speculations on Entertainment, Media, Art, and Leisure in the Deindustrial Age
Justin Patrick Moore, KE8COY

Radio is a form of technological high magic. There is something about radio that stimulates the imagination; whether it's tuning in to a distant station, or hearing something new that opens up a door onto a worthy topic of exploration, or transmits heavenly music, there is a mystery to radio that creates a strong pull over those who become enthralled by the medium. Deindustrial fiction is already under radio's thrall. Many of the stories I have read in *Into the Ruins* and *New Maps* have used radios, to the point where it has become one of the tropes of the genre. I think this points to the resilience of radio for our deindustrial futures, and I think it is worth exploring what the medium might yet become.

The word broadcasting comes to us from agriculture, and is used to describe a way for sowing seeds by scattering them over the soil rather than planting them in tidy rows. Radio is considered the first broadcast medium, for its distribution of audio to a dispersed audience over the airwaves. Though it is spread out wide as a form of mass communication, the effect of listening to radio is more one-on-one. Radio is intimate. Vibrations of a distant person's voice are converted into traveling electromagnetic waves, then get reconverted into electrical impulses and come out of a speaker to vibrate the air within a listening space. It still remains magical to me after all these years. To my mind, at its best, radio is on par with literature as a medium for sowing seeds in the imagination.

Radio can be a literal theater of the imagination. Voices, sounds, and music edited together in a pleasing or thought-provoking way transport the listener to another region. Commercial interests and market forces have put a stranglehold on the medium, however. For the most part, you have to search out the community and college stations, the low-power stations, and even the pirate stations to find programs that are willing to break the self-inflicted format categories typical of the corporate ruled airwaves. Out on the fringes of the dial, and over the edge of what is normally considered acceptable in terms of what you are allowed to do, play and say at a station, are vast portions of imaginary spectrum that remain under-explored.

These outlier shows are able to take risks that move the form forward without fear of reprisal. No one is paying them to be taste shapers by playing particular songs and they have no one to offend when exercising their freedom of speech because there are no image-sensitive sponsors paying the bills at these stations. These are directions radio would be free to go when the narrow bandwidth of acceptability imposed by advertising is removed. These under-explored areas are also ripe for retrovation. As our future societies downshift in response to being technologically overextended, the simpler decentralized infrastructure of radio will be due to make a comeback, ushering in its next golden age.

From the Golden Age to the Golden Arches

The first golden age of radio was the decade between 1930 and 1940, with some bleed-over into the 1950s when television became the next big thing. Many of the shows that emerged during the golden age were born off the backs of successful vaudeville acts who brought their talent to the airwaves. The popular pulp fiction of the time floated off its pages to be transformed into new iteration of theater: the radio play. This form of entertainment, where the voices of actors are heard but not seen, accompanied by incidental music and sound effects, is great for the imagination. Radio plays give free rein to listeners to visualize the story unfolding in their own distinct ways, similar to the way a story is imagined when reading.

Television literally tells a vision of what is in the head of a director. It takes away the chance of visualizing settings and characters. People *can* have imaginative interactions with TV but in general not much is left up to the viewer.[1] The stars of the radio comedies, soap operas, and science fiction and mystery plays migrated to TV as it became ascendant. Radio still had power but the variety on individual stations began to dissipate as the concept of the format came in vogue. Stations began to narrow their focus. Some focused on news, sports, talk, talk, talk. Religious broadcasters thumped their bibles in the studio. Music shows and then entire stations diverged into pop, rock, jazz and classical. By the 1980s heavily formatted radio stations had become moribund and varicose. With large corporations owning multiple stations in cities across the country, the sounds of the old, weird America, as heard on regional programs, began to fade, while the sound of McGovCorp cut through any static from coast to coast.

---

[1] *Twin Peaks* is an example. Enough was left unexplained to keep people enthralled by the mystery.

Thinking of all the possibilities radio has, it is a real shame that broadcasting in its commercial aspect long ago fell into such a well-worn, predictable, and boring rut. The songs heard on the air when tuning across the dial have been played so many times there are almost no grooves left on the records. Nor is talk radio exempt. No matter what a person's political persuasion may be, pundits on both sides of the aisle trot out the same plodding talking points time and again, no matter the issue at hand. It often makes me wonder what the heck the point of all the uninspired and placid propaganda blasted across the spectrum actually is; maybe it's just a form of anti-thought to occupy the minds of hungry commuters and consumers. Broadcast radio as it now stands is a depreciated spectacle spread across the spectrum. It could be so much more.

By the '80s in America, there were few places to experiment with anything off the pre-approved, record-industry-friendly playlists or talking points. If you were lucky there was a college or community station somewhere on the dial where DJs and hosts could play and do what they wanted to. Listener-supported public radio offered some variety, for a time, and in some places pirate radio scenes were (and are) active in their electromagnetic resistance to the mandates of the FCC.

Free-form radio came about as a result of the creativity of disc jockeys who followed their own muses, playing things of any genre or style, and mixing in talk and made-for-radio audio collages without being beholden to the dictates of a station manager—themselves beholden to corporate interests beholden to making money by selling time to advertisers. Big business doesn't want views critical of any of their products aired on stations running their ads, thus limiting speech and song. The McGovCorp version of radio also put the kibosh on shows devoted to particular styles. Genres such as ambient, electronica, the heaviest kinds of metal, the most independent punk and rap, and those devoted to ethnic folk music are criminally neglected on the airwaves. This lack of variety often drives some to go pirate.[2]

All the things that have normally been shunned to the far edges of the dial and overnight time-slots by McGovCorp are actually the things that could make radio great again. I think that time will come during the long descent as the high costs of television production and internet streaming skid into the obstacles of inflation, resource depletion, and waning public interest in spectacle and propaganda.

---

2 David Goren has shown with his Brooklyn Pirate Radio Map how much pirate radio is done by various immigrant and ethnic groups whose culture and communication needs aren't being served by corporate radio, driving them to play their music and announce their news on pirate FM stations. See: https://www.pirateradiomap.com/

Amateur Radio: A Real Can of Worms

Broadcast radio is only use of the technology. As a form of direct person-to-person communication, radio is a real can of worms. Not in that it causes problems, but that the worms so often wriggle forth to make claim after claim upon a person's time. Radio is the kind of hobby that can easily become an obsession and take over every aspect of your life. In the coming years those saddled with this obsession may serve to keep distant communities stitched together, support their villages and cities in times of natural disaster or manmade emergency, and otherwise have a blast rag-chewing with people across the country and all around the world.

Many new converts to the ham way of life come to it from the prepper subculture and already have a built-in mindset around the idea of short and long-term catastrophes affecting civilization. These are the people who are building stations, stashing equipment, and fortifying themselves with knowledge to pass on to others. Not every ham shares these views, of course, yet most are community-minded folk and many participate in public service events where back-up comms provide an extra safety net, should those used by police and fire departments fail. Some hams get involved in the allied hobby of storm spotting, relaying their on-the-ground weather sightings to broadcast stations to put together warnings for the wider public.[3] Others are pure techies who spend little time transmitting and put all their efforts into soldering homebrewed gear on their workbench. Others just use radio as a way to be social and have long back-and-forth conversations and roundtable discussions with their fellows. Still other amateurs just want to chase DX (distant foreign stations) whose call signs they can put into their logbook and exchange QSL cards with (postcards, often with artwork, noting station details and specifics of the exchange). DX chasers often end up with binders and shoeboxes full of these cards from friends far away. Those are just a few cans of worms available to the amateur radio hobbyist. There are many more endeavors within the hobby should you choose to open the can. These include bouncing your radio signal off the moon, learning Morse code, and talking through dedicated ham radio satellites—while we still have them, before Kessler syndrome sets in.

The many modes available for hams to operate in also allow a great variety of potential use. Every radio signal that goes over the air is modulated in some way—by voice, by the on-and-off of a tone such as in morse code, or by digital methods that connect one computer to another over-the-air, sans internet. A ham with the right setup can send text messages using radioteletype, for in-

---

[3] *When the forecasters' guild around Addleton can manage it, they should really look into some ham equipment to supersede that old phone system—see first story in this issue, "Rocketsonde." –Ed.*

stance. This toolkit can be deployed by those who wish to have a resilient web of communication when the existing web goes down (or becomes so much more full of crap than it is now that it is no longer worth the bother).

The existing ham radio network's decentralized nature is a core strength. This decentralization will help ensure that it remains viable as society shudders, shutting other doors of connection. In the golden age of radio to come, independently self-organized hams will be able to conduct on-air meetings—called *nets*—to exchange critical information, news and messages. If one station shuts down—for the night or even forever—others can remain on the air. If an important message needs to be relayed, the decentralized nature makes it more reliable, as there is no single point of failure. It is even possible, as the long descent continues, for the dedicated hobbyist to set up their own radio-based Bulletin Board System (BBS) to send email and texts over the airwaves as long as basic computers can be kept running.

Downloads From the Aether

In the 1980s, in Czechoslovokia, behind the Iron Curtain, citizen access to home computers, and their experience with them, was very different than the West. The science of cybernetics had been dismissed by the Communists as bourgeois. When the Eastern Bloc started to gander how computers were being used for strategic military and science purposes, the authorities started to change their tune. The Communist computer scientists had to roll their own systems without help from the bros in Silicon Valley. The machines they came up with would be unfamiliar to most Americans. As Communist products, most were not used as personal computers, but as collective computers for schools, institutions, and a few lucky clubs. Yet, as with so much else, western systems were smuggled in and personal systems cobbled together. An underground subculture coalesced around the exchange of information and programs, often in the form of zines and cassette tapes from amateur radio and computer clubs.[4]

Early computer programs were often stored on magnetic tape, reel-to-reels on the mainframes, and later cassettes. Engineers involved in the Nederlandse Omroep Stichting (NOS), a Dutch broadcasting organization, realized the data could be transmitted as audio over the air. They got the idea to create broadcasts

---

[4] Tangentially related is the case of "Bones Music" or "Ribs Records." These were bootleg records of outlawed Western artists pressed into used x-ray films and traded on the black market in the Soviet Union. The book to check out on the subject is *X-Ray Audio: The Strange Story of Soviet Music on the Bone*, edited by Stephen Coates, published by Strange Attractor. The shortwave radio show *Imaginary Stations* also featured a segment on bones music by Stephen Coates in a program titled "X-Raydio" first broadcast in 2022, archived here: https://archive.org/details/x-raydio-ch-292-version

where people could tape a game or program off the air and use it on their computer. Such programs gained a niche following in Europe in the early '80s. The tapes, and sometimes the radio signals, sometimes crossed over the Iron Curtain to be copied and traded.

The sound of these programs will be familiar to those who remember dial-up or those with experience of ham radio data modes. Yet the practice of broadcasting computer programs over the air stopped in the mid- to late '80s as computers sped up. The audio technique of encoding a program didn't work for 16-bit computers. Cassette storage was out, and floppy disks were in.

A similar situation as existed in the Eastern Bloc during the Cold War could come to the West during the course of its decline. As people are forced to adopt older technologies, a small hacker and ham subculture could trade programs by broadcasting them over radio, to be taped onto cassette and loaded into existing refurbished computers taken out of the basements and garages of avid geeks. Enthusiastic retrovators could do the work to get these vintage computer systems running. When combined with ham-radio-style BBS systems an older '70s to mid-'80s style of radio-based internet could be kept up for at least some time during the long descent among the technically adept. Mimeographed zines could provide documentation of best practices.

More recently some ham radio operators have also been known to repurpose wi-fi routers to create line-of-sight internet wireless mesh networks. Cory Doctorow's novel *Someone Comes to Town, Someone Leaves Town* features a punk rocker who runs a dumpster diving operation, salvaging computers to set up a mesh net in Ontario. In the interim before the internet itself is gone, such a mesh net may be useful to those who wish to escape the increasingly censorious panopticon of social media, but want to remain online and able to share files and information.

Such alternets to the web as it is known today, and other imaginative uses of radio, await the energized hobbyist in its next golden age.

A Free Radio Republic

In the absence of a legitimate government, pirate radio is always an option.[5] The barriers to entry in the broadcasting game aren't as expensive as one would think, especially if one has a more modest area they wish to cover. If they do their pirate radio on the shortwave part of spectrum they can reach a wider, though smaller audience, due to the propagation effects. Shortwave radio pirates remain active on the air year after year.

---

5 As the author of this column I do not advocate any illegal activity—the ideas presented here are for informational and speculative purposes only.

Piracy has existed since the beginning of radio broadcasting and there is no reason to think that it will ever stop as long as radio is around. Pirate radio has every reason to continue to proliferate. When certain groups of people and types of programming are kept from speaking their minds and playing the music and sounds related to their culture on the corporate blandwaves, it has even greater appeal. One way of looking at pirate radio is as a "Media Squat," a term coined by media theorist Douglas Rushkoff. Instead of squatting in an empty unused house, the media squatter takes up residence on an unused frequency. Contrary to the popular conception of squatters, it isn't a given that they will wreck the place they are squatting. Many make improvements. The same can be said of squatting on a radio frequency and putting out better programming than the stuff trickling down from the big guns. From my study of the current pirate radio scene it seems the FCC is much more liable to hunt down transmitters on the FM and commercial broadcasting portion of the spectrum than they are the sporadic efforts of shortwave pirate radio hobbyists.

If you want to put your own station on the air without breaking the law, though, there is another option. Part 15 of the FCC regulations ruling electronic communication do allow for smaller FM and AM broadcasting with limited outputs of power and strict guidance for interference with other stations. But small is beautiful, right? These types of stations can potentially reach a block to a few blocks in a city neighborhood, and can be quite fun to run with a minimum of equipment and technical know-how. Certain patriotic groups have even advocated setting up networks of Part 15 stations. Synchronized to a single source, or daisy-chained together, they would play the same material, creating a low-tech network capable of blanketing larger areas — given enough stations.

Pirate radio and Part 15 stations can be used to create healthier radio ecology than the current monocropping.

Signals Intelligence

The radio hobby is such a can of worms that this column can only scratch the surface of all the possibilities that await those who jump down the rabbit hole into its wonderland. Everything from shortwave listening to radio scanning can be folded into the hobby. For folks who are a bit mic-shy and don't want to talk on the air themselves, these latter two may be useful places to start. Shortwave listening is one tool for getting information from around the world when other sources fail. Even in times when there is no emergency or crisis, listening to news and views from other countries, hearing their music, and learning about their culture is an engaging past time, as is chasing DX.

On the local front, having a scanner radio capable of picking up police, fire, aviation and other signals is a good way to keep tabs on what is going on in your community before the media picks it up and puts their spin on events. Having a scanner will be especially useful to monitor situations in events of civil unrest and natural disasters. I find scanning to be somewhat depressing, as listening to people get arrested or hearing another call to the fire department about an elderly person who has fallen isn't always my idea of a good time. Yet the practice of listening in to this kind of radio traffic does have a definite use. If you enjoy trains or aviation, it's pretty easy to pick up comms from rail yards and air traffic control.[6] These are just a few of the doors that can be unlocked with a scanner. Those who become adept at scanning can end up being sleuths of the airwaves, tracking down frequencies and listening to government agents, utility companies, and private businesses all as a way of gathering information and signals intelligence.

Carrier Waves

In the next golden age there will be numerous ways to interact with radio, similar but different to how things are done now. Business as usual in the radio industry won't be an option. The cracks in legacy media are already widening, and beneficial weeds are starting to claw their way through. With any luck these early colonizers will make things ripe for a bountiful media ecology that nourishes the soil of the imagination to regenerate the medium so its many untapped possibilities are open for new uses in a declining age.

Local and hyperlocal broadcasting may once again rise up, giving voice to bioregional concerns and culture. On these shows a truly diverse range of programming could be encouraged. As television falls away actors could find a new home in the revitalized world of the radio drama. The home use of scanners can keep listeners informed of the goings on in their neighborhoods in times of quiet and emergency, allowing them to make up their own minds about events. On the national level, a smaller number of larger AM and shortwave stations could be used to tie the bonds of North America and other continents together. A robust ham radio scene, intertwined with the remnants of the hacker subculture, may give rise to an alternet web of radio based communications. And on these carrier waves the seeds of America's next great culture may be broadcast across the land.

---

6   *Any deindustrial down-and-out who can at least manage to hang on to a scanner will have a trick for getting from one city to another that wasn't available to Great Depression hoboes: listening in on yard operations is often the best way to find out which trains are going where, and in fact lots of present-day trainhoppers carry scanners for exactly that purpose. —Ed.*

Re/sources:

American Radio Relay League (ARRL). https://www.arrl.org
- → For those in the United States, this is a great resource for all things amateur radio, from getting licensed, to finding a club, to setting up your first ham station and getting on the air.

DeFelice, Bill. *Part 15 Broadcasting: Build Your Own Legal, License-Free, Low Power Radio Station.* Self-published, 2016. https://www.hobbybroadcaster.net/resources/free-part-15-radio-broadcasting-ebook.php
- → Bill DeFelice has put together a wonderful website at hobbybroadcaster.net devoted to Part 15 broadcasting, with many articles and resources to help people get started.

English, Trevor. "You Could Download Video Games From the Radio in the 1980s." Interesting Engineering (website), Mar. 8, 2020. https://interestingengineering.com/science/you-could-download-video-games-from-the-radio-in-the-1980s

Finkelstein, Norman H. *Sounds in the Air: The Golden Age of Radio.* New York, N.Y.: Scribners, 1991.

HF Underground. https://www.hfunderground.com/board/index.php
- → This site offers the description, "Shortwave Pirate Radio In North America And Around The World, And Other Signals That Go Bump In The Night." HF Underground is more of a message board where people who listen to shortwave pirates post about what they hear. Active radio pirates have been known to hang out and lurk on the boards.

Lewis, Tom. *The Empire of the Air: The Men Who Made Radio.* New York, N.Y.: Edward Burlingame Books, 1991.

Maly, Martin. "Home Computers Behind the Iron Curtain." Hackaday (website), Dec. 15, 2014. https://hackaday.com/2014/12/15/home-computers-behind-the-iron-curtain/

Phillips, Utah. "Radio: The Story of Radio from Crystal Set to 'Sandman the Midnight D.J.'" Originally broadcast on KVMR, Nevada City, Calif., 2008. https://www.thelongmemory.com/loafers-glory-episodes
- → The episode in question is number nine of *Loafer's Glory*, but any of Utah Phillips' amazing slices of radio are worth taking the time to listen to.

Radio Society of Great Britain (RSGB). https://rsgb.org/
- → Our friends across the pond tell us great things about RSGB. It is also open to international members. For those in the UK wishing to get licensed the RSGB will provide the relevant details.

Reitz, Ken, ed. *The Spectrum Monitor.* https://www.thespectrummonitor.com
- → A monthly online PDF magazine covering "Amateur, Shortwave, AM/FM/TV, WiFi, Scanning, Satellites, Vintage Radio and More." Each issue is a hefty chunk of knowledge, history, how-to, and reports from radio active writers.

WB Rice

And There Was

And Grandfather said …

ONCE, THERE WERE cities and buildings
And there were houses and roadways
There were schools and libraries
And there were museums and showplaces

There were factories and machines
And resources and products
And there was concrete and asphalt
And steel and metal and glass

There were contests and competition
And there was buying and selling
And there were profits and dividends
And costs and expenses

There were families and gatherings
And there was food and water
And there were smiles and laughter
And there were songs and singing

And there were rulers and leaders
And congresses and committees
There were experts and advisers
And there were considerations … and discussions … and negotiations

And there were maneuvers and other such activities
And there was reasoning and there were rationales
And there were agreements and affirmations
And there were thoughts and actions
And explanations and implications
And there were consequences and justifications
And reverberations and ramifications

And there were fallacies and fables
And stories and myths and narratives
And there were hopes and wishes
And there were good intentions and bad faith
And there was belief ... and disbelief

☉

AND THERE WAS vanity and pride
And there were lies and deceit
And foolishness and wishful thinking
And corruption and hypocrisy and double-dealing
And there were illusions and fabrications

And there was dissatisfaction and discontent
And dissonance and discord
And downturns and diffusion
And disintegration and degradation

There were shortages and outages and failures and waste
And things rotted and deteriorated
And there was contamination and infestation
And there were catastrophes and quakes and cataclysms
And there were explosions and eruptions and disruptions

And there was fog and smoke and dust and confusion
There was shouting and noise and madness
And there was nakedness and fleeing and terror
And there was sickness and hunger and desire and need
And there was fear and anger and tears and sadness

And things were broken and broken down

And there were losses of every kind

And there was death

And there was … blood

And there were piles …

Of rubble … and bodies and bones ……

☉

AND … THERE WAS strength … and courage
And there was wisdom and knowledge and patience
And there was willingness and cooperation and kindness
And there was friendship and kinship

And there was shelter and comfort
From the wind and storms and turbulence

And there was a time and place
And the seasons came … and left … and came again
And the sun and the moon and the stars watched

And there were miles and miles and miles …
And wave after wave after wave …
And hours and days and months and years …
Of distance and dimension …
Of length and height and depth …

And there was silence ……

And there was grace and mercy

And there were humans and animals and other creatures

And the earth turned … and things continued

STORIES

Clint Spivey

Rocketsonde

THE FIELD WAS EMPTY but for Howard and his massive paper lantern. The stars above burned fuzzy through the lingering wildfire smoke of a late-summer sky. At this late hour, not even the crickets or cicadas were to be heard. The only sounds were the tiniest gurgle of the parched river beside him. If his plan worked, he'd be able to gather data not seen in over a decade.

Howard worked quickly to unfurl the paper shell, nearly two meters in diameter. He'd spent weeks researching and then creating a strong enough heat source necessary to propel the lantern to sufficient heights while also carrying the required weight. A tiny cake of sawdust soaked in kerosene sat in the middle of a thin wire housing. Attached by a five-meter string was his payload.

The tiny wooden block was identical in weight to the sensor and transmitter he planned to use if this test succeeded. The lantern unfolded, the kerosene cake in place, all there was to do was light it. He pulled out his Zippo.

"C'mon, work," he muttered to the empty night, hoping the exhortation wouldn't jinx his attempt. The lantern rose, an eerie glow illuminating the blue-and-white paper sides. Had he done it? Access to upper-air data across the region would transform the Weather Guild's products from a hobby of compiled surface observations into something resembling a functional forecasting system.

As the lantern gained altitude, a tiny string unspooled from beneath. Howard held the block in his hand, ready for the lantern to take it aloft. If it rose, then he'd succeeded with a lantern robust enough to carry a radiosonde.

The lantern lurched. Its graceful ascent in the still air suddenly shifted from the added weight, curving away from the riverbed to the east. Toward Addleton.

"Shit, shit!" Gone were any dreams of success. Howard sprinted beneath the lantern, which was still rising despite its ominous, off-center tilt. Maybe it was fine. Maybe the weight on that side wouldn't cause problems. Helpless to do anything more, he whispered prayers to whoever might be listening.

Seemed no one was. The lantern erupted. Its ghostly glow blossomed into a fireball as the paper caught fire. It burned for a mere second before being consumed. Like all such paper lanterns, this was by design. The problem now was the falling sawdust-kersosene cake. Also by his own design, it was meant to burn long and hot in order to propel the lantern upwards.

"No, no, please no," Howard pleaded between breaths as he sprinted to keep up. The tiny flame streaked down, straight toward the roofs of Addleton's sleeping residents.

"The whole damned coop!" the woman said, stamping her foot with the final word. "Thirty hens gone! Because this sumbitch likes pretty lights."

The packed courthouse mumbled their agreement with Isabel's statement. Nearly all Isabel's neighborhood had been roused by the fire. Even more had turned out when Howard had been brought forth as its cause. Now, with Venus still burning in the morning twilight, those who hadn't helped fight the fire were at least going to stock up on some good gossip-fodder for being woken so abruptly.

Howard stood in front of the crowd beside the mayor, the sheriff, and the volunteer fire chief, as well as the city council members who had pushed their way forward to show they were part of the town's leadership in such emergencies.

"The hell were you thinking?" Sheriff Connor asked. "You some kind of pyro getting your kicks?"

"No, no!" Howard raised both hands in hopes of placation. "It was an ... experiment." The statement was met with grumbling and shaking heads.

"Lighting a fire in the sky," the fire chief, Acevedo, said. "All alone. And you didn't even think to let us know ahead of time?" He gestured to his fellow firefighters who had also jostled for a front-row seat to the proceedings.

"I thought it would be safe. Paper lanterns always burn up before they hit the ground."

"Bullshit," Isabel said. "Burned strong enough to ruin my whole coop. Who's going to pay for this?"

"Are *we* getting paid?" one of the firefighters asked to nods of his compatriots.

"Sounds a lot like arson, to me," Sheriff Connor said. "You're gonna see a jail-cell for this."

"Not before I get paid," Isabel said.

The volunteer firefighters again demanded their own compensation.

Mayor Mackie stepped into the fray, quieting the crowd with a single raised hand. "What kind of experiment were you conducting, exactly?" she asked.

The crowd, almost as one, craned their necks forward.

"An upper-air sounding." Howard went on to explain the need for more in-depth data to improve his forecasts. With spotty electricity and even spottier internet, Addleton and the surrounding towns often found themselves without any reliable meteorological information. The Weather Guild tried to make up for this, but, limited to charts created with surface data alone, could only produce the most rudimentary forecasts. The vast wealth of information above their very heads—temperature, pressure, winds—data that only a few years before was easily obtained—was now as hidden as hieroglyphics lacking a Rosetta. As he continued his explanation, his gestures grew more animated, his voice higher and more exuberant until the crowd, unsure whether their local Guild forecaster was a fool, simply listened.

"The thunderstorms especially," he said to the group. "With upper-air data, me, and everyone else in Addleton, Quartzville, the whole region, could give concrete information regarding storms."

He saw a few nods in the crowd. With an uncoupled jet stream alternating between massive blocking patterns and ferocious storm fronts, all appreciated the real threat that unpredictable weather had become.

The mayor moved closer to the crowd, her voice a little louder so all could hear. "And how, exactly, did you plan to achieve this with a ... Chinese lantern in the middle of the night?"

"I need to get a sensor in the air. High enough to measure temp and pressure at least throughout the column. The lantern burned up quick enough. But, well, I made the fuel source to burn longer in order to gain enough altitude to get the sonde—the sensor—aloft. But it came down instead before burning up."

He looked around in hopes his explanation had worked. And while he mostly saw confusion and anger, a skinny guy in a ball-cap gave him a sucks-to-be-you shrug.

"It was just a test," Howard said, looking at the ground. "Helium might as well be non-existent these days. Since balloons are out, figured I'd try a lantern."

The crowd grumbled. Isabel reiterated her demands for compensation, as did the volunteer firefighters complaining of lost sleep dealing with Howard's mess. Mayor Mackie and Sheriff Connor stepped aside to discuss the issue while the city council members tried to look important. Howard waited.

"You burnt down a house?" The voice on the other end of the line was incredulous.

"A henhouse, actually," Howard muttered. The phone had been ringing when he arrived at work following the morning's events. Someone in the mayor's office had informed his superiors in the capital.

"With a lantern? The hell you doing, celebrating Chinese New Year early?"

Howard went on to explain to his boss--a normally friendly woman named Treharne--what he'd been attempting. After he finished, the line was quiet for several moments.

"Listen," she said in an icy tone. "You are in Addleton for one reason. And that is to show that the Guild has value. Not to experiment. Not to innovate. To prove that we are necessary. Do you know they're threatening to cancel our contract there?"

Howard hadn't. Though being banished from Addleton back to the city wouldn't exactly break his heart. As if reading his thoughts, Treharne continued.

"Need I remind you that your own employment with the Guild could be at stake? You volunteered for this assignment. If you can't even do your job then maybe the Weather Guild isn't for you."

Howard winced. He'd been a decent forecaster once. When there existed tools and technology enough that forecasting required little more than a solid internet connection.

These days? In this economy? He was happy just to be employed. If he lost even that ...

"I understand," Howard said finally. "I was just trying to ... never mind. It won't happen again."

He waited a long moment before realizing she'd hung up. Sighing, Howard did the same.

"I want all of it gone," Isabel demanded while gesturing to the burnt remains of her hen-house. "When the guy comes to give me an estimate on a rebuild I want this place spotless."

Howard nodded and tugged on his work gloves. The sheriff had decided not to lock Howard up. Better he work off his debt for Isabel's property in addition to financial compensation for her lost hens. So, at five o'clock in the morning, with a freshly drained bank account, Howard found himself wading into the wreckage, which still stank of burnt feathers.

"Same time tomorrow," Isabel ordered as he finished his first shift. Still employed with the Weather Guild--at least for the moment--he was needed at work. His punishment extended to times beyond work hours.

"Something smells good inside," he said, trying for a placating tone.

"Eat on your own damn time." She slammed the back door.

The bicycle ride back took around twenty minutes. With fuel shortages and the subsequent high prices, someone like Howard was relegated to bicycle travel. These days, he and other cyclists had the roads mostly to themselves.

When he'd first arrived to the town of Addleton, Howard had expected another meth-ridden town of abandoned storefronts and desolate streets. Instead, the town was seeing a sort of resurgence. Having come out on the other side of cold-turkey withdrawals from cheap fossil fuels, the people found themselves biking and walking whenever possible. This had led to the main-street shops and markets, once desolate casualties of hyper-capitalist big-box stores, blossoming back to life.

A growing cottage industry of delivery services had also sprung up to serve those too elderly or infirm to make the trek downtown. Even now, Howard saw several young people loading bicycle baskets and trailers with groceries. Others chatted in groups, their bikes loaded and ready to go.

Howard resisted a stop at Baker's Row despite the enticing smell of fresh bread. So named for the sandwich shop, two bakeries, and brewery in a line, the adjacent businesses all shared enough need of similar ingredients that they'd formed a sort of co-op. The reality of Howard's much depleted finances overruled thoughts of breakfast despite his growling stomach. He headed to work.

"Sorry man," Howard said to his assistant after arriving. "I tried to hurry."

"No worries, man," Sandum said from his desk in their office.

The Guild paid for the use of a two-story house. The two had their own rooms on the first floor while sharing a kitchen and bathroom. The second floor was dedicated to work.

Sandum had only recently become a Guild member. He'd been sent to assist Howard in Addleton after the office had been established. While larger cities boasted more robust staffs, the two of them were all the town had. Sandum handled the office during nights while Howard covered observations and forecasting during the day. While not technically a forecaster, Sandum had hopes of training to become one eventually.

"Anything big happen last night?" Howard said while looking over the hourly weather observation sheet.

"No one else tried to burn down the town."

"Good to hear. Any internet?"

"Oh yeah," he said. "The unicorns got it working last night."

"Right. Get some sleep."

After Sandum headed downstairs, Howard checked over the younger man's hourly weather observations from the previous night. He confirmed the most recent recorded pressure with their wall-mounted barometer. He then checked wind speed and direction on a small, Guild-provided automated observation system with its own solar setup. Finally, he checked the marine barograph against the current surface pressure. Little more than an upright, clockwork-wound cylinder wrapped in paper, its rotation and tiny inked needle provided a quick look at pressure tendency. After several months together, he trusted Sandum's observations, but checking them helped Howard better understand the current weather situation.

Even back in the city internet had been spotty. In a small town like Addleton, it might as well be non-existent. Many in Addleton had their theories. Sabotage by hostile foreign nations. Government conspiracies to keep rural populations ignorant of nefarious schemes. Aliens. Howard suspected something much more mundane. Desperate telecoms scraping meager profits by abandoning the hinterlands was his best guess. Whatever the cause, Addleton struggled simply to maintain phone lines with the outside world.

With no internet, all Howard and his colleagues in the region were capable of producing were basic surface charts. By comparing current observations for Addleton with those from Guild members in surrounding areas he'd be able to plot the surface analysis for that day. The phones were still up even if the internet wasn't. And though they occasionally lost even *those*, he and the other Guild members were usually able to conduct conference calls to coordinate their forecasts.

After brewing a pot of tea, Howard settled in, picked up the receiver, and dialed the number for the daily weather conference call.

"I'm not changing my forecast, Trent," Howard said, the phone receiver tucked between shoulder and neck while he sorted through previous surface analysis sheets.

"No way winds are gonna be that high," came Trent's response. The others on the call kept silent, likely munching metaphorical popcorn for the argument.

"Are you not seeing this gradient?" Howard asked, comparing his previous two charts. "Hell, I'm probably calling the winds *low*."

"Dude, we've got the fireman's muster this weekend."

"All the more reason to let them know weather's gonna be shit."

"Winds aren't going to be that high," Trent repeated, as if persistence mattered to Mother Nature. "If they see your forecast higher than mine they might cancel the event."

"As they should. Unless you want plates full of potato salad flying through the air."

"Help me out, man. Can't you *do* something?"

Howard looked upwards in the eternal lament of the forecaster. How many times had he heard similar requests back in his Navy days? An outdoor command event. Live music. Hell, the Admiral's golfing. We can't have shitty weather. Don't you know how much money has gone into this? And the most ridiculous of all, echoed by Trent sixty miles away, Isn't there something *you* can do?

Sure. Let me give Mother Nature a call. She owes me a favor. That's totally how a global atmosphere containing billions of eddies and currents blasting across continents works. You're a go for the command barbecue, sir.

"I ain't changing my forecast, Trent. Bite the bullet and tell them the wind speeds. Let them decide whether to hold their event in a near-gale."

The line crackled but otherwise remained silent. Howard shrugged. Not his problem. He kept silent until the forecaster from Quartzville chuckled and began sharing her observations from the previous night.

"We're definitely going to see those winds," she said, after reading off her station's obs for everyone on the line to record. "It's all the same data we're looking at."

And it was. Their combined dozen or so stations, spread out across around four hundred miles, offered a sizable enough dataset to create at least a basic forecast. They couldn't do more than combine their surface observations, then extrapolate twelve to twenty-four hours out from there, but it was better than nothing.

Long gone were the days of mammoth super-computers churning out charts to ninety-six hours and beyond. Howard had heard some still existed in the world. But they'd been switched over to more "important" functions than forecasting, such as crypto mining and AI chat research. If the Guild wanted proper weather charts now, they had to create their own.

Which was precisely why Howard was so keen on getting a radiosonde aloft. If each station had access to upper air data, the guild would be able to produce far better forecasts. In addition to vital skew-T analyses for each station, it might be just possible to create upper-air charts sets for their region. Having even a basic idea of 500-millibar troughs and ridges, or 850-millibar temperature advection, would elevate the Guild's products from lick-a-finger-in-the-wind to actual usable data out to forty-eight hours, if not longer.

Howard slumped into his seat. His lantern had been an interesting idea. But it had also almost gotten him thrown in jail. He was broke and still stunk from clearing the wreck of Isabel's henhouse. Perhaps innovation in the new world was foolish. People were giving up their cars, something previously unthinkable. Maybe it was time he did the same with his dreams of better forecasts. While he was staring out of the window into the late summer sky tilting brown with distant forest-fire smoke, the doorbell rang.

"Saw you this morning," his visitor said with a small nod.

"Oh, yeah," Howard said remembering the skinny man from the morning of the fire. "Travis, right?"

"Yep. Heard you talking about weather balloons."

Travis had the kind of rail-thin figure that in no way implied weakness. He could have subsisted on Pabst Blue Ribbon and cheeseburgers and retained a physique like Iggy Pop in his prime. His lower lip bulged with tobacco. Brown spit pooled in the soda-bottle spittoon he carried.

"Why's it gotta be a balloon?" he asked, leaning over Howard's surface chart.

"Well, I guess it doesn't." Howard filled in the pressure, temp, and winds for the spot on his chart corresponding to the town of Bastion before connecting the 998 isobar behind the node. "It was just the way we used to get upper-air data. Launching balloons."

"Y'all actually did that? Them big weather balloons?"

They had. Howard recalled his time in the Navy. Lugging cumbersome helium bottles aboard ship for a deployment. Half the crew would turn out, it seemed, to watch them send up balloons. Ditto for anytime they practiced ashore.

"So you need to get something high up. Some serious altitude?"

"The higher the better," he said, completing the 994 isobar with his pencil. He began working on the 990.

Travis spat into the plastic bottle. "Why can't it be a rocket?"

"That's my setup." Travis gestured to the still taking up most of the immaculate barn. Travis had invited him over to his place that same evening. After turning over to Sandum and grabbing a quick bite, he'd bicycled to the address Travis had given.

Howard had expected a rifle-toting family barefoot in coveralls. Stray dogs and toothless dueling banjo players. Basically any rural stereotype his city-boy mind could conjure. Instead, well maintained grounds surrounded a barn containing a massive still gleaming with copper and steel.

"How'd you make this?" Howard asked, feeling the smooth metal. "Was your family into ... moonshine, or something?"

Travis scoffed before spitting into his bottle. "That what you think? Some old family roots of rum-runnin' and bootleggin'?"

Howard turned to look at him, suddenly embarrassed for the assumption. "I just thought—"

"I *was* a welder." Somehow the whole sentence came out as one word. "Worked in a distillery. Maintained rigs bigger 'n this for years. When it came time to build my own, wasn't much more than following the diagrams in a book."

"Cool."

Travis nodded.

"But, you really think you can make ... I dunno ... rocket fuel."

Travis shook his head. "Not fuel. Candy."

Never before in Howard's life had he considered those twain words would meet.

"Rocket ... *candy*?"

"Yup. Never made it myself, but knew some guys into model rockets when I was a kid. Shouldn't be too hard."

Travis led him away from the massive distillation apparatus to an office. A dusty computer—likely used as little as the one back at the weather office—sat on a desk piled with notebooks, sale slips, and other paraphernalia of a bustling business. A shelf crammed with books and binders took up an entire wall.

"Technical manuals, mostly," Travis said while looking through the titles. "Other 'n that I don't really read."

"What *do* you do here?"

"Alcohol," he said, pulling a large binder from the shelf. "High percent stuff. Sanitizer and sterilization for clinics and vets mostly." He looked up from the binder's glossy pages to Howard. "And moonshine."

"Seriously?"

"Yeah, man, I was just messing with you before. I make some decent hooch. You probably had some if you ever been to Jose's."

Howard frowned. "So what's the catch?"

"Catch?"

Howard shrugged. "Why do you wanna help me? What's in it for you?"

"Does something have to be in it for me?"

"I mean, that's been my experience in this town."

Travis looked up before answering. "Well. I've had my share of projects blow up in my face. Guess I just recognized the same look when I saw you'd almost burnt down the town." Travis shook his head. "I know the feeling. Here we are." He turned the binder toward Howard.

And there it was. Different recipes for homemade rocket fuel. And one in particular nicknamed "rocketcandy."

Howard frowned. "Listen. I appreciate the offer. But I'm kind of on thin ice as it is." He explained his superior's insistence that he do no more than his job.

Travis nodded thoughtfully while occasionally adding to his spit-bottle.

"Doesn't mean *I* can't build a rocket, though, does it?"

Howard smiled. "I suppose not."

The next morning saw Howard reporting to the fire station at five o'clock AM. While the city had indeed decided to pay the firehouse for their efforts at extinguishing Isabel's hen-house, they wanted—and got—a piece of Howard's punishment pie.

"And after the toilets, mop the floors," Chief Acevedo had ordered. "Then head to the kitchen. Stove needs cleaning."

So it was that, for the first time in nearly thirty years since his time as an airman in the US Navy, Howard found himself scrubbing someone else's shitter.

The wind howled that night. House-rattling gusts that implied an atmosphere gone mad. And while there were no storms alongside it, that wasn't why Howard went to bed smiling. Those gusty winds would be blowing all weekend and Trent still refused to change his forecast lest he upset Quartzville's planned picnic. Sometimes even better than verifying a forecast was verifying it when someone else doubted you for it.

"That's about as aerodynamic as a brick," Travis said, turning over the radiosonde in his hand. He'd popped into the Guild shop to chat. The styrofoam square was about six by four inches and an inch thick. "The weight won't be a problem. But no way this is going up on a rocket."

The radiosonde was US Government surplus. Howard had secured it from one of several pallets the Weather Guild had acquired but as yet hadn't gotten around to getting aloft. Supposedly there were warehouses of the things. Forgotten once helium had become scarcer than reliable internet.

"We don't need to get the whole thing up. Just these." He broke open the styrofoam to reveal the water-activated battery, the antenna, and the actual sensor itself. A pliable, delicate strip of metal that measured temperature and pressure as it ascended aloft. Relieved of its case, the largest section was the battery at about an inch and a half square.

"That might be doable," Travis nodded before spitting into his bottle, already two fingers full of foul spittle. "Could pack the whole thing in with the 'chute. Take your measurements while it fell. But how you getting the data?"

Howard pulled a strip of paper from the radiosonde's styrofoam side. An inch wide and resembling some ancient tickertape, it unfolded to about a foot long and was arrayed with a complex series of holes like an ancient computer punch card.

"This links it to the receiver," Howard said. He led Travis to a closet and lugged out a metal box the size of an ice-chest. The dented, olive-drab case opened to reveal the controls. He'd dragged it along with the rest of his gear when the Guild sent him to Addleton.

"You slide the tape through here," Howard said, demonstrating the procedure though the receiver was powered down. "It reads the tape when pulled through that slot, then syncs to the sonde. You launch it. Then wait for your data."

Travis nodded. "So all we have to do is get this"—he shook the radiosonde—"up in the sky."

The passing weeks saw approaching fall continuously interrupted by scorching late-summer heat accompanied by brief but intense thunderstorms. Howard and Sandum spent their days alternating between calling out thunderstorm warnings, heat advisories, and air-quality warnings from wildfire smoke to Addleton's residents. They were going to need a new sling psychrometer with all the extreme heat baking the town. And though the wildfires remained thankfully distant, the smoke and its lung-irritating effects had no problem tormenting Addleton's residents.

During those evenings when violent thunder rattled the windows, Howard thought of upper-air data. On the rare occasion the internet was up, they could access radar data to watch for storms. Other times, when the storms moved in a line, they relied on the surrounding towns reporting their movements in order to warn the locations in their path. Often, this allowed an hour or less to prepare. But they didn't always move in lines, sometimes exploding into being with little warning at all.

And though counterintuitive, worse was when Howard called for thunderstorms and none appeared at all. One could only cry wolf so many times before the locals began to doubt.

Howard sighed while trying to focus on his book, an old sci-fi series he'd loved as a kid. Travis was confident he could craft a large enough rocket to contain the sonde, but he had his own responsibilities. He still provided vital goods to the town, to the point that Howard had begun to feel bad about monopolizing so much of the man's time in what could easily become a hopeless endeavor.

The window flashed blue. Howard waited mere seconds until the thunder crackled into a deafening roar. He frowned, and closed the book. Reading old sci-fi always depressed him for several reasons. Not least of which, he'd once believed in all the genre's promises.

He set down the book and retrieved a thick binder from a shelf. Sitting down to his desk, he opened it up, and smiled. His old Navy rating manuals, Aerographer's Mate Second Class, Volumes One and Two. He turned to the section on upper air data.

He'd once laughed at the procedures and gear the manuals described. What had before seemed quaint technology from the '50s and '60s, left in the manuals for reasons unknown as the meteorological world had shifted to supercomputers and the internet, was now as valuable as a recipe for Greek fire.

He read through the various methods of upper air soundings the Navy had once employed, including hydrogen-filled balloons for use in certain latitudes. He'd once considered such a technique given that electrolysis seemed at least feasible to produce hydrogen, but quickly abandoned the idea after some back-of-the napkin math. Likely a good call seeing the damage he'd caused with a simple paper lantern. He turned to the page on rocketsondes and paused.

All of this because of a lack of helium. He remembered supermarkets and floating balloons. A literal *element* once so accessible and cheap it was a children's plaything. Now, just another vanished link in failing supply-chains.

It suddenly struck him that *this* might be the new science fiction. No rocket trips to space but rocketcandy-fueled models attempting to stay ahead of climate chaos. Building what was needed with what was available to try and keep society afloat another day.

Howard closed the manual and switched off the lamp. Lightning lit the room not a heartbeat later.

"A foot-rub," Isabel said, revealing a wicked smile.

Howard stopped raking. "No," he said. "No!" He dropped the rake. "I'm done. Hear me? I've paid my dues!" he shrieked in an embarrassingly high tone. Damn the mayor and damn the sheriff. He was through letting some miserable old shrew torment him.

Isabel just grinned before saying, "Well it was worth a shot. Can't blame a girl for trying." She gestured to the back door. "Come inside. I've got some biscuits ready."

"No!" he yelled before registering what she'd said.

She shrugged. "Suit yourself." She slammed the screen door in his face.

Howard winced. Those biscuits smelled good.

His shift at the firehouse was less jovial.

"Fold," Chief Acevedo croaked while nodding to several hampers of laundry. The man looked as if sleep was something remembered from another time.

"Long night?" Howard asked, dragging a hamper toward a table.

Acevedo stared for an uncomfortable several moments. Howard turned his attention to the firehouse's socks and shorts.

"The Dalton place," the fire chief finally said from behind him. "Tree came down last night in the wind. Half-dead pine."

Howard kept his attention firmly on his work.

"Came right through the kids' room. Missed the crib. Didn't miss the bunk beds."

Had Howard ever met anyone named Dalton? He didn't think so. Addleton still boasted something like fifteen thousand residents. And at that moment, several of them were now dealing with a shattered children's bedroom and a ruined life.

Howard turned, waiting for the accusation. The usual anger at weather directed to the weatherman.

It didn't come. Acevedo stared out a window.

There were always stories. Of emergency responders. Trauma nurses. Doctors. Anyone often in the company of death and their gallows humor to maintain sanity in the face of calamity. *That*, Howard could have dealt with. A sick joke about dead kids and fallen trees.

What was harder, and infinitely worse, was seeing a fire chief shaken into silence.

"It's just too damned windy," he finally said. He looked once more at Howard, shook his head, and left.

Had the chief been disappointed in Howard's forecasting? Or just the daily powerlessness against an atmosphere boiling with more heat than it had seen in millennia?

Probably both. Howard returned to the laundry.

"Holy shit, man," Howard said while examining the rocket. Travis grinned before taking a drink from his beer.

The bar was loud with a typical Friday crowd. Average Jose's on Baker's Row wasn't the only bar in town, but definitely the most happening one. The place had long since grown profitable enough that Jose only tended bar when he felt like it.

"How'd you make this?" Howard handled the rocket with care.

"Wasn't too bad, actually." Travis went on to explain how he'd found some people who knew model-rocketry well enough to give pointers. With his welding knowledge and abundant scrap leftover from his still, he'd been able to craft something lightweight yet fairly durable.

"The problem's gonna be finding it again after we use it," Travis said. "I take it you need more than just one of these?"

"Yeah, you could say that." Howard handed back the rocket before taking a drink of beer.

"Oh my God, is that yours?" A group of younger people at the next table had noticed Travis's work. He perked up while explaining it to the group.

Despite the interest of several attractive young women listening to Travis, Howard's thoughts wandered. They had a rocket. Next was a test. Howard didn't relish asking for permission after his lantern incident. Nor the response from the Guild if they found out what he'd been doing. But even if they succeeded, then what? Who'd pay for more rockets? Who would even build them?

The lights and music vanished. The sudden hush of silenced patrons lasted only a moment as the realization settled in of another power outage.

A massive bell clanged to life from the bar following hoots and whistles from the patrons.

"Light 'em up!" Jose yelled.

Howard frowned as Travis produced a match and lit the candle at their table. Soon, light glowed from several frosted red glasses at each table as patrons hurried to get theirs lit.

"We have a winner!" Jose shouted while pushing forward a massive jar of liquor, a coiled snake soaking at the bottom.

Howard had thankfully never been last to light his candle the few times he'd been at Jose's during a blackout. Groans arose from the losing table as shots of habusake were brought out.

Travis slid a shot glass in front of Howard. Apparently his standing had only grown with the table beside them upon learning he supplied Jose with booze in addition to building rockets. Whiskey slopped onto the candlelit table as shot glasses clinked together in cheers.

Howard joined in but remained silent, his thoughts lingering on fallen trees and bunk beds.

"No." Sheriff Connor crossed his arms. "Absolutely not."

Howard and Travis stood before the sheriff, Chief Acevedo, and Mayor Mackie in her office. Travis held his completed rocket prototype. "We're pretty sure about her," he said, raising his work. "Got a 'chute worked out and everything."

"No." The sheriff shook his head before pointing at Howard. "I wouldn't trust him with a water balloon. Let alone a rocket."

The mayor held up a hand. "I thought you said you'd launched weather balloons in the past. Is this something different?"

The room went quiet as they looked at him.

"We used these, too," Howard said. "In the Navy, I mean."

"You did, personally?" the mayor asked.

Howard admitted that he hadn't actually ever launched a rocketsonde.

"And the Guild?" she asked, arching an eyebrow. "I spoke with a ... Treharne, I believe her name was. Does she know about this?"

"This one's my idea," Travis said, coming to the rescue.

"Doesn't look too bad," Chief Acevedo said. He gestured to Travis, who handed him the rocket. "How long a burn ... or whatever, you looking at on this?"

Howard once more considered unemployment as Travis explained the details. He didn't relish thinking of what other work his meager skill set might allow.

"We just need a test," Howard finally said. "That's all we're asking for. But this might just work."

Howard gaped at the crowd for their launch. Sheriff Connor looked frantic while, strangely, Chief Acevedo and his guys examined the rocket setup with enthusiasm. Mayor Mackie artfully handled the crowd, her messaging turning the launch into a community event. She bragged about the progress it represented and what better forecasts might mean for Addleton.

Several local shops had stalls with refreshments a few hundred yards from the launch site. Nearly all of Baker's Row was represented. Jose in particular was doing brisk business with his scantily clad staff serving from kegs.

"Quite the crowd," a voice said behind him. Howard turned to see Isabel, her smile only slightly less mischievous than normal.

"Uh, yeah."

"Brought you something." She handed him a warm basket covered in cloth.

"Really?" Howard asked, accepting her offering. The biscuits smelled delicious. "Thank you."

As much as he'd have liked to witness the event, Howard was needed at the office. While searching for his bicycle among the dozens of others in the parking area, he spied a lone stall. Some kind of bake sale. Proceeds going to the Dalton family. Dozens waited patiently to make a purchase. Howard located his bike, and paused.

Contrails blossomed above. It was strange to think that somewhere, somehow, planes still flew in the sky. He looked once more at the stall raising money for the Daltons before departing.

Back at the office, Sandum had the bulky receiver plugged in and ready to go. At the launch site, Travis had loaded the sonde and was just waiting to activate the battery. All they had to do was give the signal over walkie-talkie.

"Soak the battery," Howard said into the tiny radio. After receiving confirmation, Howard pulled the ticker-tape matching the sonde's frequency through the receiver. A few moments later, the large metal box chirped to life, the little tune confirming a sync between receiver and radiosonde.

"Ready on your end?" Travis asked.

Sandum looked at Howard and crossed his fingers.

Howard hurried to plot the data. Once upon a time he could have simply copy-pasted the values into a computer-program and several different thunderstorm indices would have appeared in a matter of seconds. Now, he was grateful just to have the data, hand-scrawled by Sandum from the tiny receiver display that resembled an '80s alarm clock. Howard pulled out the ancient skew-T chart, a calculator-sheet whose creator Howard felt deserved a Nobel Prize, and began plotting the data.

It had been years since he'd plotted one with actual data. He'd practiced though. In preparation for this day.

Normally with balloons, data was plotted from the bottom of the chart. With a rocket, the data was reversed, the sensor only deploying with the parachute and measuring temperature and pressure during the descent. Howard located the lowest millibar value corresponding to the rocket's highest achieved altitude, and began his plots from there. With a prepared lesson for Sandum on the marvels of a skew-T upper air analysis ready upon his lips, Howard began.

He needn't have bothered.

They'd barely reached one thousand feet. Impressive for a first-time model-rocketry attempt, no doubt. But for a forecast? Howard had temps and pressure up to barely the 850-millibar level.

He sat back, looking at his paltry little skew-T chart, nearly nine-tenths of it blank due to such little data.

"What is it?" Sandum asked.

What had he expected? Thirty thousand feet and up to the 200-millibar level on their first attempt?

"This is ... worthless," Howard said, deflated. "With such little altitude I have no clue what's happening in the upper levels. I can't even get proper thunderstorm indices from this. No Total Totals. Maybe a Showalter Index, if I just pluck a 500-millibar value from mid-air, but ..." He looked at Sandum and slumped. "All this work for nothing."

Sandum stayed quiet, only the receiver singing its remaining connection to the radiosonde breaking the silence.

Both turned as the downstairs door opened followed by footsteps up the stairs.

"Dude!" Travis said while slapping Howard on the back. "You shoulda seen it! Whole town was cheering."

"That's great," Howard said with far less enthusiasm.

"The place went nuts," Travis continued, oblivious to Howard's defeat. "Half the elementary school is out looking for the rocket. Jose promised a free round to the family of the kid who finds it and I'm throwing in two bottles of hand sanitizer."

Howard nodded.

"Mayor's here with some lady from the *Gazette*," Travis said as the front door again opened. Mayor Mackie's clear voice floated up from the entrance.

"What?" Howard looked to his skew-T sheet. He'd failed spectacularly. And apparently the entire town thought otherwise.

"Well done." The mayor reached out a congratulatory handshake. "I'll be sure to inform the Guild of your success. Addleton will definitely be renewing our contract."

Howard looked to Sandum, who simply shrugged while trying to hide laughter.

A woman with a notepad and pencil introduced herself from the *Addleton Gazette*. Before Howard could answer she rushed into several questions.

Travis winked while the mayor beamed.

Howard looked to his work. Even a guessed Showalter Index was better than nothing, he supposed. He thought of the jet he'd seen earlier. Back in his Navy days, they'd once utilized pilot reports for weather. Could they do the same again? A pirep could give pressure at altitude. Enough, perhaps to calculate a thunderstorm index. Something over nothing was certainly an improvement from before.

And the town of Addleton seemed happy. Happy with Guild services rendered. Which meant Howard's employment might just be secure. His spirits sufficiently lifted, Howard answered the reporter's questions while explaining the need for similar data from the surrounding towns.

"We're looking to go higher," Travis said. "And build more."

"Possible export industry for Addleton, Mayor?" the reporter asked.

What *if* every town had their own source of data up to the 850-millibar level? Would it solve every problem of a murderous, boiling atmosphere? Not likely. Would an 850 chart be another tool to at least help *deal* with such calamity? Absolutely.

Howard turned to his skew-T, which looked much less worthless than before. Maybe working with all you had *was* the new science fiction. And what Howard had, right at this moment, was data up to the 850-millibar level.

It was a start.

Wesley Stine

Luna the Kitten

Second Daughter

I T IS NO SIMPLE THING to relate the beginning of my misfortunes.

Of what shall I speak first? How I spent my best years in pursuit of an empty relic of a foolish age? Or how I was thrust out into the streets with no one to speak for me, when a bankruptcy ended my apprenticeship one year early? Or how, at age sixteen, I was apprenticed to a bookbinder in the first place? Or how I was born the second daughter to a poor family on the western marches of the Denver Kritarchy? For none of these ills would have befallen me, had I not already been afflicted by the one that came before.

From our earliest years it was Kira whose pretty face the grownups praised, Kira for whom our parents bought a chiffon dress even though it meant pawning our father's fowling piece, Kira whose marriage they were always anticipating. My own name was hardly mentioned except when they were telling me to do some chore.

I well remember the time, in the fall of 2236, when they thought they had found a suitable match for my sister. He was a comely lad from Fort Collins, nineteen years old to Kira's sixteen, a third son, but from a wealthy enough family that he could have started a respectable household when his share of the inheritance was joined with Kira's dowry.

He made a good show of himself in the village of Netherlin, catching fish and ducks on the lake, proving himself an able carpenter when he helped us raise a new wind turbine, dancing with Kira in a most lively fashion, and showing up the local boys in their games of wrestling and volleyball.

Then my parents found out, with the aid of a distant relative in Fort Collins, that this youth had lied about being a virgin—he had already slept with at least two girls in his hometown, one of whom was known to carry the rotting germ.

For this there could be no lenience; an armed mob met by night and drove him out of Netherlin, not even seeming to notice that they were doing violence within a mile of the bailiff's keep, and that any one of them could have ended up on the gallows if they had been less lucky than they were.

"It was harsh," my father said, "but fair. I may be poor but I'm not stupid; I know as well as anyone what the rotting germ can do, and no amount of looks or charms will make me marry my *eldest daughter* to someone who might have it."

I wondered for a long time afterward if he had said it that way because he *would* have married his second daughter to any suitor, rotting germ or not, who was willing to take her off of his hands. And as the days and years went by, I came to feel more and more certain that the answer was yes.

The next year my parents finally found a husband for Kira, and they married her off in a great feast. I was not happy during the feast — it was not just that I disliked the groom (although I did), it was also the knowledge that my parents had borrowed money to pay for the wedding, and that I would be spending much of the next six months cooking and cleaning in some manor house or another to earn back the cost.

At least my parents did not shoot off any rockets. Whenever there's a birth or a marriage in the bailiff's household, they celebrate by launching colored rockets a little after dusk. And I've heard it said that the money spent on just one of those rockets is enough to feed a poor family like my own for a whole week.

With Kira's marriage attended to, and our brother (who would inherit the land) still very young, my father and mother had time to deal with the unimportant question of what would become of their second daughter, the one with no dowry.

I expected that I would have to learn a trade. If, after my apprenticeship, I found good employment and saved money fast enough, I might meet a young man in the same situation, willing to look past the fact that my best years were half gone, so long as the two of us had enough substance to start a household of our own.

I was apprenticed to a bookbinder in Bolder. One day I was told by my father that the contract had been signed and deposited; two days later I left my birthplace behind with only two loaves of bread and the clothes I wore. And thus I turned my back on Netherlin and the snowy mountains all around it, and walked the morning's journey to Bolder.

The only pleasant thing I can remember from my apprenticeship is the books.

Our master and mistress were austere; they gave us few privileges and beat us often. The food was plain, the beds were hard, and on the coldest winter nights we had to share our room with the chickens and the pig. We were not allowed to have instruments of music, nor could we ever visit taverns, so for us the only music in those years came from the high-walled convent on the other side of our street, where at certain hours the sisters climbed their tower to sing psalms.

But the books made all of these miseries half-worthy of being borne. Now, if you are an apprentice bookbinder, your master and mistress probably don't want you to *read* the books, but they can't really stop you, either—at least not if you're discreet about it. And so in my five dreary years at the bookbinders', I spent most of my time imagining my myself in a hundred other worlds more colorful than my own.

In the Red

There are two kinds of work that a bookbinder gets asked to do. The first is to bind new books, fresh from the inkpress. Most of the books we bound were of this sort, but because they came in large, identical batches, each copy earned only a little money.

The second type of work is to restore old books, repairing the spines and covers and sewing the loose pages back into place. The price per volume is much higher, because so many people have books that there is only one of, perhaps in the whole world, and they are willing to open their wallets to save these books from decay.

Even so, we still had to turn away about half of these people, because sometimes it's the pages themselves that are perishing—cracking or turning to sawdust because they were made of cheap paper to begin with—and there's nothing a bookbinder can do to put them back together again.

For the first two years of my apprenticeship, my master and mistress found enough of these two kinds of orders to keep our balance sheets in line. But from my third year onward, their losses grew ever deeper until they finally exhausted their credit and declared bankruptcy. The next day we apprentices found ourselves on our own, without house or money or trade, and none of the other bookbinders were willing to take us on.

It was of course in their own interests to turn us away. Why accept a girl with only one year left until she leaves you and becomes your competitor, when there are plenty to be had who will serve you the full six years?

Nor was there a place for me with my family in Netherlin. My father had died by then, and my brother-in-law was head of the household. He had no affection for me, and Kira managed to be even worse, along with my mother. "We've provided for you long enough," she said. "Whatever made you think you could just come back and live off our charity again? Is paying for your brother's education, and looking after three grandchildren, not enough for us already?"

And though I tried to explain that having skills wasn't the same as having a license, and that I may as well just be another housemaid for all that the law cared, she did not have the patience to listen. So the next day I was back in Bolder.

The sisters at the convent were kind enough to let me stay with them while I thought about what to do next. And that is when I decided to try something all too audacious—a lawsuit.

I had bound seven or eight newly printed legal manuals during my brief career—they were just about the commonest sort of books that were produced in this day, what with bailiffs and judges being so important—so I knew how to file a case.

I was going to petition the judge to order the bookbinders' guild to either apprentice me to a new master, or else admit me in my own right. I would say that to do otherwise would violate my constitutional rights. After all, it would be very unfair for me to get nothing at all for my five years of labor, despite my already knowing the skills of the trade. (It was of course a bit of a stretch to say that this had anything to do with our country's constitution, but I knew from reading a few history books that much bigger stretches had met with success in the past.)

I spent the next twenty-six nights researching and preparing the lawsuit. The sisters let me use their library, though by day I had to earn my own living by working as a cleaning wench at a nearby tavern. At last my documents were all finished and in order, with everything in two neat, handwritten copies—one for the superior judge, and one for me to keep.

The next morning I walked to the grand building where the judge held court. I had actually been inside it once before, when my family were called as witnesses in a land dispute, and even though I had only been six years old, I could still distinctly remember the majesty of the place: the plush carpets and the broidered robes and the gilded furnishings and (what was most rare and wonderful of all) the electric lights. And I remembered the decorum, and the bowing, and the delicate tapping of heads on the floor, and the oft-repeated dictum, "To hear is to obey."

This time I did not actually go into the courthouse; I only handed a silver megadollar to the guard at the gate, and dropped my envelope full of documents into the bronze box beneath the great carved inscription about how the doors of justice are open to everyone.

But while I was there I met another would-be plaintiff, the leader of a team of four lawyers representing the farmers and ranchers near Vrain Creek, on the northern edge of Bolder's jurisdiction. They had spent nearly a year gathering evidence and preparing a suit to force the city to double the number of marshals patrolling near the creek, so as to protect their clients from banditry.

This lawyer told me that, despite all the work they had done, he suspected that the odds were still three-to-one against their winning in the end.

Next to that, it was clear enough that my own puny lawsuit didn't stand a chance. So I was not surprised when my feeble cry for justice was never answered with even a summons to a preliminary hearing.

After two more months had passed, I fully gave up on the law and all that went with it.

The bookbinding shop still stood, full of books, right across the street from the convent, a tantalizing reminder of what might have been. It was locked because of the bankruptcy; the magistrate had ordered that the property remain untouched until it could be sold and the proceeds divided among the creditors. But I was of the opinion that what the creditors had lost in the shop's failure was a trifle compared to what I had lost.

So one night, I broke in through a place where I knew that the wall was weak, scooped up some of the books that I knew to be most valuable, and hastened away under cover of darkness. I was well outside of Bolder by the time that dawn broke and the sisters sang the day's first psalm, and I did not stop moving until I reached the Springs, ninety miles to the south.

Swapping Stories

It was during my flight southward that I began calling myself Mara; of my birth name I spoke no more, lest my crime be discovered. And thus began my career as a book peddler.

I made my first sale in a village called Moñumin, a little north of the Springs.

A woman named Dina lived there; she had a large courtyard adjacent to her house, and she kept a tiny library in the room overlooking it. She had obtained her books after contemplating how useless it was for children to be in school six hours each day learning to read (as the judges and bailiffs required all throughout the Denver Kritarchy) if most of them would never handle a book outside of their classrooms. And so Dina had created this small library for children, where those with nothing else to do could gather after school let out, to read on their own (if they were able) or to sit on the stones of the courtyard and be read to.

To Dina I sold an illustrated children's book by a man named Kipling. It was quite a silly book, a fable (if I remember right) about a crocodile and a curious young elephant. In exchange for it I got three quarters of a megadollar, and Dina let me stay with her three nights, and eat at her table, and in the afternoons we read to the children together.

It was a few days after that, in Bolder proper, that fortune briefly smiled upon me, and I made my first real trade.

I had sat down to show my wares to an old man who was a book collector. He said he had little money to spare, but since I had some volumes that he wanted, he offered to trade book for book. It became clear as we were negotiating that he didn't really know what most of his books were worth, and I ended up getting three treasures from him—Churchill's *My Early Life,* Prescott's *History of the Conquest of Mexico,* and Neidhardt's *Physiology of the Bacterial Cell.* And in exchange for these I gave him a pair of thick, trashy fantasy novels with their oh-so-gaudy covers.

After this I realized that I could be a book peddler forever, if I managed to find enough people who could be persuaded to sell low and buy high. And for a long while afterward, I managed just that.

It was not easy. I had to wander all over the lands that used to be Colorado, and a few times I even hazarded a journey outside the Kritarchy's bounds, to places like Peblo or Shaián where outlaw chiefs bore rule. Sometimes I happened upon three or four good customers in a row, and enjoyed many nights sleeping in soft beds, and many days dining at their tables, on steaks and roast lamb and cherry pies and spiced wine.

But at other times I went months without making a sale, and I was constrained to eat scraps from compost bins, or to rest beneath eavesways on cold and rainy nights, thinking, sometimes, of the brothel-houses (for the nearest one was never far away) and the warm and well-fed women inside them, and being tempted to do as they did, if only for one night. But I never yielded to the temptation; the chill of night would be gone in the morning, hunger would be forgotten when I made my next trade, but to get the rotting germ, and to spend years wasting away as my flesh turned to fluid from the inside out—that was a risk that I was never weak enough to take.

One evening in the fall of 2245, when my purse happened to be about half full, I was dining in a tavern in Fort Collins when the place suddenly burst into a ruckus. A salvager had told his tablemates that, some years earlier, he had been working the ruins of a nuclear power plant way off to the east in Nebraska, and a moment later the other guests had thrust him out, lest they be struck down by his contagion.

After a while I slipped out to find the man. I knew better than to think that nuclear poisons (whether they still existed or not) could be transmitted like a virus, but I figured that if I brought him food and drink, he might reward me with a little silver.

He did, and I also got an earful from him about "mindless superstitions" and the people who spread them. He explained how there was no danger at all in salvaging at a nuclear plant—the isotopes that could kill you on sight were long gone, and you would have to drink tainted water for months or years to get harmed by what was still there.

And even *that* wouldn't have been a problem if the engineers who had built the plants had also been allowed to build "deep repositories" for their waste. But their plans had been thwarted by "activists and protesters" who thought that nuclear power was evil through and through, and that anything that let the masses think it was safe—such as a functioning waste repository—only compounded the evil.

"It was a bit like if you had a man who goes around his village saying that nobody must ever build thatched roofs, since they're too vulnerable to fire, but when the other folks don't listen to him, he turns arsonist, and goes out setting fires himself, under cover of darkness, just to prove to everyone that he was in the right."

The salvager went on like this for a long time, complaining about all the superstitions and wrong beliefs that most people held about the past, and how they made his life so much harder than it needed to be. Most of what he said was forgettable, but at one point he gave a long discourse on thinking machines, and how they had existed, briefly, in the twenty-first century. He said they could beat human champions at games of skill like chess, and they had achieved feats of inventiveness, such as designing the CHEMTRACE berry, that were beyond the abilities of human engineers.

The thinking machines had also written books for the enlightenment of mankind, and though most of the books had since been lost, one of them could still be seen at the library in Fort Morgan.

And that was how I entered upon this quest—upon my most foolish errand.

I knew full well that there was little future for Mara the travelling book peddler. It was an exciting career at times, but all too often it took all my wits just to not starve. But all of that would change if I found a book written by an artificial mind, whose intelligence (as I supposed) must have exceeded that of human authors as much as the old mining machines, whose colossal hulks still lay rusting on the mountainsides, exceeded the digging powers of human hands. If I could find this book, and get possession of it, and bring it to Denver, and sell it to someone who knew what it was worth, then my days of poverty and irrelevance would be over.

Foolish Errand

I searched for the mysterious book for four years before I finally found it, and I suppose that at no other time has a woman (or a man) spent four years so wastefully.

The first place I looked for it was Fort Morgan, at whose library the salvager had said the book was to be found. And there *was* a library there, but it was in a very poor condition, with big cracks in the roof, and most of the books were rotting away on account of the rain. When I made my profession known to the keeper of the place, he let me search his collection freely, saying that anything could be mine if I offered something useful for it.

The man was so absent-minded that I could easily have robbed him, if I had wanted to. But in truth there was little of value there; most of the collection had been sold, almost thirty years earlier, to libraries in Aurora and Fort Collins, with no records of what had gone where. But I did see, in a worm-eaten recordbook, a mention of "texts generated by artificial intelligence," from which I inferred that the salvager had at least been close to the truth, when he told me that the book was to be found in Fort Morgan.

I went to Aurora next. But the keepers of that city's library were under a judge's order to let no one in except on government business. And so the only information I could get about its contents came indirectly, during my ordinary trades with the city's book collectors, as I wheedled them for their recollections about what they had seen in the big library, back when it was of a more public character. I was unable to figure out if my book was there or not, and so I continued my quest.

I of course could not follow this one trail all the time; I still needed to eat, I still needed to get into the good graces of wealthy book lovers who would lavish rewards upon anyone who could fill a gap in their collections, and I still needed to resupply myself at the expense of others who had inherited old books without knowing what each volume was worth.

Thus I continued to lead the kind of life I have already described, a life of luxury mixed with poverty, but mostly of poverty. I knew the unpleasant feeling of waking up one morning on a warm and feathery mattress, and lying there a few minutes as I thought about it being my last day with the patron who had provided it, and how it might be weeks or months before poor Mara fell asleep on another such bed. I endured hunger and thirst, rain and snow and the summer's scorching heat. I was robbed, once, but to my good fortune the thieves took only my money and not my books—if good fortune you call it, when you preserve for yourself the means of pursuing a mad end.

The library of Fort Collins, which I visited the following spring, was not in the city itself, but in a nearly-empty satellite village which had once been home to a university of forty thousand students. Nowadays it was all a grazing ground for sheep, with only two buildings still in use out of hundreds and hundreds. One was the library itself, and the other was an absurdly tall football stadium, within whose walls the present population of fifty or so shepherds had built their village, to better protect themselves from raiders from the north.

I wondered, as I crossed this desolate place, whether it might never have fallen to ruins if our ancestors had paid more attention to whatever it was that the thinking machines had had to say. Perhaps the electronic minds that had mastered our strategy games, and guided our engineers in their greatest labors, would have been able to guide us toward building a more durable world, if only we were willing to listen.

Perhaps they still could. Perhaps if I found the mysterious book, I would be rewarded with more than riches. Perhaps future generations would honor me for helping reveal to them a better way to live.

But when I finally searched the library of Fort Collins, I found myself disappointed yet again. The librarian told me that, if any machine-written books were ever there, they would not have met the criteria to be kept after the purge of 2218. There was a list of who had purchased the excess books in that year, but it only gave the name of each buyer, the sum paid, and the number of books sold — not their titles or authors.

So once again I was back to following thin leads, chasing blind hope as again and again I went into a place thinking "perhaps I will finally find what I am seeking," and came back out thinking "perhaps the hints I have discovered here will be useful."

And so it continued for four years, as I wandered all over the lands that are ruled out of Denver, from Wellingden in the north to Fort Carson in the south, from Lyman in the east to Brecken in the west, sustaining myself by ordinary trading, but making no real progress toward a settled life or an end to my poverty — not when my every spare moment was consumed in my quest for the book written by an electronic mind.

If it was only the hope of future wealth that sustained me, I do not think I would have kept up my search that long. But every day that I awoke in hardship — beneath a leaky roadside canopy, or in a roach-laden shack of an inn, or with my stomach empty from two or three days of hunger — I kept myself going by imagining a time when fewer people would have to live this way, thanks to the knowledge that I was about to set free.

And on the few days that I enjoyed luxuries, in the opulent households of the men and women who took interest in my books, I could not help but look at all the marvels around me, and imagine what wonderful things we might learn from an artificial mind that had been built in a time when everyone, rich and poor alike, had all of those marvels and more. Perhaps — I must admit that I dared to hope this — perhaps finding the book would give our leaders the clues that they still needed to rebuild such a world.

As fervently as a Texan mystic hopes to enter the Courts of the Two Ladies, or as the sisters at the convent in Bolder dreamed of seeing the New Jerusalem, so too did I hope and dream of finding even a scrap of an oracle from the long-lost thinking machines.

And the cruelest thing of all was that, in the end, I found what I was searching for.

At an old military site a little north of the Springs, there stood a half-collapsed library, where long ago, boxes upon boxes of books had been frantically gathered from all around, then suddenly abandoned. The library was now guarded by only two marshals and the librarian herself, who told me that the books on the shelves were there to stay, but the books still in the boxes were to be sold, by order of the nearest bailiff, to any visitor who offered a dime per book.

The librarian gave me a small lantern to light my way as I walked the dark halls of the decrepit building. And how lucky I was to find that one of the shelves was filled with large blue binders full of neat, handwritten lists of the books in each box, lists that gave both their titles and their authors!

I tried imagining the day—by now more than a century in the past—when the lists were made. It must have been during the base's frantic final moments, when the soldiers were preparing to withdraw eastward.

Their leaders would have known about the collapsing front in Texas, and the Latin troops' plans to cross the Red River and march on Ocesí. But perhaps the common soldiers did not know this; perhaps they only knew that they had been ordered to count and list the books in each newly arriving crate. The work was tedious, but it gave the men something to do other than consult their fears, and it also kept up discipline—it reminded them that a soldier is always soldier, and a soldier keeps track of his inventory.

Not that it was a very useful inventory. The books had no military focus; they seemed to have been gathered at random from the nearby city without even being sorted by genre. Each box held classics, textbooks, trashy novels, children's stories, histories, legal tomes, and just about every other sort of literature that I had seen during my perambulations.

I perused the lists in the binders until I spotted a book authored by someone, or something, called the *Modern AI Literacy Project*. Its title was *Luna the Kitten*. I rushed over to the boxes, glancing at the numbers scrawled on their sides until I found the right one. Then I pried open the box's lid, and shuffled through the books with bated breath, tossing the ones I didn't need onto a large heap.

And then I found it: *Luna the Kitten*. Its cover and its introduction both said that it had been written by artificial intelligence. And so, after restoring the other books to their place, I went to the front desk, paid the meager price, and rushed out the doors with my new treasure.

Then I opened the book and read it. I knew already that it was a short book, and I suspected that it had been written for children, because of its title, and because of its lavish illustrations (drawn by a human being, not by another computer).

Still, I kept my hopes up longer than I should have. I told myself that the machine that wrote *Luna the Kitten* must have had something very important to say to its audience of children. And I told myself that this message—whatever it was—would be enough to tide me over until I could find a similar book for adults.

But all these fair expectations faded away when I actually read the book, whose text hardly seemed worthy of a six-year-old. It was a trite book, a trivial book, a book that would fit right in among the silliest and most useless tales in my friend Dina's forlorn little book-house.

Luna the Kitten

Once upon a time, in a small village nestled in the mountains, there lived a curious kitten named Luna. Luna was a playful and mischievous little thing, always getting into all sorts of trouble.

One day, Luna spotted a beautiful cuckoo clock hanging on the wall of the village square. The clock was made of gleaming brass, with intricate engravings and a sparkling gemstone in the center. Luna's eyes were drawn to the tiny bird that emerged from the clock every hour, singing a sweet and joyous tune.

Luna couldn't resist the urge to catch the bird. She crept up to the clock, her paws making soft, muffled steps on the cobblestone path. She pounced, trying to grab the bird with her tiny paws, but it always managed to fly out of reach just in time.

Frustrated, Luna sat back on her haunches and watched the bird as it flew back into the clock. She cocked her head side to side, studying the mechanism with a look of intense concentration on her face. It was as if she were trying to understand the inner workings of the clock with the same intensity as an alchemist studying the Philosopher's Stone.

As the hours passed, Luna became more and more determined to catch the bird. She tried every trick she knew, from sneaking up on the clock to using her sharp claws to try and snag the bird as it flew out. But no matter what she did, the bird always managed to evade her grasp.

Finally, in desperation, Luna decided to try something a little more unconventional. She remembered hearing the old village wise woman talking about a special type of brownie that was said to give the person who ate it enhanced senses and reflexes. Luna had always been a little skeptical of the old woman's stories, but she figured she had nothing to lose at this point.

So, she scurried over to the wise woman's cottage and begged her for one of the mysterious brownies. The old woman hesitated at first, but eventually relented, handing Luna a small, fragrant square. Luna sniffed at it suspiciously, then tentatively took a bite.

To her surprise, the brownie tasted delicious—like a combination of chocolate and mint, with a hint of something spicy and exotic. Luna gobbled it up eagerly, then bounded back over to the cuckoo clock, her senses heightened and her reflexes sharp as a razor.

As the next hour approached, Luna crouched down, ready to pounce. The cuckoo bird emerged from the clock, its song ringing out across the square. Luna sprang into action, her paws a blur as she chased the bird around and around the clock.

Finally, with a triumphant yowl, Luna caught the bird in her paws. It struggled and squawked, but Luna held on tight, her eyes glowing with triumph. She had done it—she had caught the elusive cuckoo bird.

As Luna carried the bird back to her home, she felt like she was walking on air. It was as if the rings of Saturn themselves were lifting her up, carrying her away on a wave of pure joy and accomplishment. She knew that she would always treasure this moment, and the memory of the day she caught the bird inside the cuckoo clock would stay with her forever.

Answers and Questions

I had to read *Luna the Kitten* two or three times before I was certain that I wasn't overlooking some ingenious message—before I admitted to myself that I had only found another one of those talking animal stories, and an especially banal one at that. But eventually I admitted it.

And so, the next morning, I left the book with Dina, who was still reading to the children of Moñumin each afternoon. Then I hurried away northward, setting a brisk pace, since I knew that if I didn't keep moving I would probably break down and cry.

The next year was probably the bleakest year of my life. The summer was short and rainy; the winter was long and cold. I still wandered the roads of the Denver Kritarchy, following the trade of a book peddler, because it was the only trade I knew. But I did my work drearily, without the hope of gaining anything more than a brief reprieve from hunger each time I made a sale.

About a year after I had found and disposed of *Luna the Kitten*, I went to Bolder to sell two hymnals to the convent on the very same street where I had done my apprenticeship. The sisters of course recognized me, but so much time had passed that I was no longer in danger of being punished for what I had done there so many years earlier. Judges and bailiffs are aloof, and can often be cruel, but they're still willing to tie their own hands over things like the statute of limitations.

During my stay at the convent, I met a woman named Sara, who had lodged there while on business for the Order of Afterlings. The Afterlings are a sort of wandering scientists, so called because they arose after the great scientific discoveries had already been made, and their mission, as they see it, is to keep the old knowledge from being lost to the ravages of time.

The coming of an Afterling to an obscure place like Bolder is usually welcomed, for the Afterlings are able physicians and engineers, they know how to test the earth and the water for poisons, and they can tell us when a piece of farmland is deficient in a certain nutrient, and what crop must be grown there to restore balance.

Sara knew that I was a book peddler the whole time that we were there together, but I was shy about the more unique parts of my life story, and it was only on my last evening at the convent that she found out about my long search for, and eventual discovery of, *Luna the Kitten*.

Sara found the whole thing fascinating. She claimed that she already knew the basic history of artificial intelligences, but she had never read a whole book written by a machine, and she was very curious about what my book had said. And so I summarized the story as best I could, hoping that Sara might be able to tell me why it was that the men who built the thinking machine had put their creation to such an absurd use.

"That sounds like a typical thing for an AI to produce," said Sara, after I finished my summary.

"Typical? What do you mean?"

"Oh, just the style of the story. The words are pretty, and they're all perfectly put together, but the plot is so clichéd. So imitative of what human authors were doing — I mean, what human authors of the less creative sort were doing — around that time.

"You've got this young and enthusiastic protagonist, who's also a natural troublemaker. She's trying to achieve a goal that seems impossible. She has to work really hard at it, and come up with a unique plan, but after a great deal of effort, she solves the unsolvable. And her triumphant feelings will last forever.

"Nearly everyone who was writing for children back then was doing some variation of that."

I thought of the hundreds of children's and young adult books that I had seen over the years, and I realized that Sara was probably right. As the twenty-first century dawned, the broad-minded literature of earlier times had given way to a narrow field of ersatz morality tales, in which the moral always seemed to be that there aren't any limits to what the protagonist can do, as long as he or she wants it badly enough, and is willing to throw caution to the wind.

I nodded slowly. "The children's books were like that," I said. "At least, they were like that near the end, right before the presses stopped running."

"Now for this Luna story," said Sara. "That simile about the rings of Saturn is so unique I figure it must have been in the prompt. And the one part that seems like magic unless you know a bit about the recreational pharmacology of this region — well, a lot of children's books had things that were meant to go right over the children's heads but get a good laugh out of the adults. But for the most part it's a fine but rather mindless imitation. Typical of what artificial intelligence can produce."

"So you're saying," I said, "that the machine was actually stupid? That it only pretended to be able to think?"

"In a way," said Sara, and afterward paused for a moment.

"The people who expected AIs to think the way that you and I think were all disappointed, in the end. It was a brutal feeling, for a lot of them, since it had almost become a religion. They'd stopped believing in the old gods, and they really thought they were going to build themselves a new god, something to bow down to and worship, something that would tell them how to live out their dreams.

"But there were just as many other people who understood the limits of AIs, and who put them to good use. And most of the AIs that were ever made were actually quite good at whatever single task they were built for."

I sat there confused for a while, since what this Afterling had said so far had left me with more answers than questions. What did it mean for thinking machines to be "stupid" and "clichéd" but also "very good at what they were built for"?

"Isn't it true," I said, "that they beat human champions at chess, and designed the Chemtrace berry? Don't those things take a lot of brains?"

"Oh, that," said Sara. "Well, the AIs did have artificial neurons, lots and lots of them, so in a way they were copying a human brain. But they really only copied a small part of the brain — the part that recognizes patterns.

"Just think about how you can look around and see the earth and sky and trees and birds and bugs and things, and you just know what they are, and you don't need to think about it. Well, that's what AIs did — they could be trained to recognize patterns in data, and see when objects were similar to each other, and put them in the right categories. But they couldn't really think about the objects."

"That still doesn't make sense," I said. "Now you're making them sound like small children, who can say 'That's a tree!' or 'That's a bug!' but can't say much else."

"Ah, but they were very good at putting things into the right categories.

"Take chess. You could train a network to play chess by showing it millions and millions of game positions, and labelling all the ones where white eventually won, and the ones where black won, and the ones that were draws. The machine would learn to match positions to outcomes, and it did this better than a human being could. So when it played chess, all it had to do was look at the thirty or so moves it might make next, and rank the resulting positions from best to worst."

Next, Sara explained the CHEMTRACE berry. It so happened that at this very moment there were CHEMTRACE berries growing in the convent's garden; they grew on small bushes and were shaped like large blueberries, but their hue was a very plain white. If you purified their juice, then added a little of it to some water, it would turn bright colors if the water was polluted—blue for heavy metals, green for actinides, red-gold for chromium and arsenic, and so forth. The berry, which had to produce many carefully designed chemicals in order for this to work, was a marvel of genetic engineering, and everyone knew it had been designed by artificial intelligence.

But in Sara's explanation, this just happened to be one of those lucky things that required only the special kind of mimicry that AI was good at. She explained how in nature, there were millions of proteins, all made from polypeptide chains by means of the genetic code. Every living thing was built from its own unique set of proteins. The patterns by which a certain chain folded itself into a certain protein were too complicated to be understood by the unaided human mind, but a machine could be trained to follow them, and to predict a protein's structure from its genetic sequence.

Then, by running the program in reverse, the scientists could make artificial proteins that changed shape on contact with a specific atom or ion, and not any other. Within the CHEMTRACE solution, there was an enzyme protein that bound to lead, one for mercury, one for plutonium, one for americium, and so forth. When the enzyme was activated by binding to its target, it catalyzed the production of a dye of the appropriate color. By this means, a single atom of pollutant could trigger the creation of hundreds or thousands of molecules of dye, so that very tiny contaminations—even a few parts per billion—could be detected.

"But it's an exaggeration to say that machines designed it," said Sara. "It was people who came up with the idea, people who gathered the data to train the machine with, and people who worked very hard to figure out how to insert all those new genes into the berry bush's DNA in just the right way to make sure everything worked."

Then, as if I needed more proof that AIs, on their own, were stupid, Sara explained how a program like the one that composed *Luna the Kitten* had once been asked to list all of the United States Presidents by their birth years, which it did. Then it was asked to list the first thousand prime numbers, which it also did. But if you asked it to list all the presidents born in prime numbered years, it gave a bunch of wrong answers. The program could spew out data, and sometimes the data was accurate. But it couldn't think about the data.

I sat there for a while afterward, not sure what to say, and I did not hide my emotions well, for Sara could tell that I was very ill at ease, almost indignant, though toward whom or what it was not clear.

"That book," she said, "were you expecting it to tell you something more useful? To give you answers, about why history happened the way it did, or how we ought to live our lives here and now?" She almost smiled with amusement.

"I sort of was," I said, feeling bashful, since I did not like admitting that I had anything in common with the ancient builders of thinking machines — with the people who imagined that they could build new gods for themselves out of copper and steel and silicon.

"Well, if you knew what AI was, and how it worked, and what its limits were, you wouldn't have expected that."

Then, a moment later: "It's not rational to be angry at a tool for having limits."

That was about the last that we discussed of the matter. I left the convent early the next morning, just as two of the sisters mounted the tower and (without raising my spirits in the slightest) sang that day's psalm:

The idols of the heathen are silver and gold, the work of men's hands.

They have mouths but they speak not; eyes have they but they see not.

They have ears but they hear not; neither is there any breath in their mouths. Ah—

They that make them are like unto them; so is every one that trusteth in them.

Bound at Last

I am now middle-aged. It has been years since I gave up on my old and hazardous occupation, years since I stopped traveling alone on the roads and trading books, years since I gave up my hopes of ever earning a respectable sum of money, or of finding a husband.

Yet my tale is not wholly a tale of woe. I have at last settled down; I am bound to a community now, and to a place. I have my sisterhood, for I live at a convent in Larkspur, very much like the one in Bolder that was the scene of so many of my earlier affairs. And in between simple meals and prayers before the high altar, I still do the work that I love. For there are many books here that must be attended to, both in my convent and in the abbey a half-mile away— many volumes that need repairing, and many others that are valuable enough that I get asked to copy them.

It seems that, so long as you are willing to work and pray, then even if there is no place for you in the outer world, there is a place for you here.

At the abbey there is a crew of deaf people, nearly two dozen in all. The abbot has learned how to communicate with them by signs, and he has instructed them in leatherworking, so that they spend their days making saddles, and stirrups, and strapsacks, and shoes.

They seem happy when they're working, and I have to let go of my own anger whenever I'm with them. It seems that Providence has seen to it that, whatever my own misfortunes may be, I can't go long without being reminded that there are others who struggle with weaknesses of which I am wholly free.

It is a curious thing that when you imagine twenty deaf leatherworkers speaking in signs as they ply their trade at their long tables, you think of them doing it all in silence. But in truth they are very loud. For they are always tramping about the room, and noisily dragging the furniture from place to place, and bringing their tools down with a crash or a thud. To people like me they seem clumsy, but their work itself is neat.

At first I tried learning all of the signs, but even after I had memorized about thirty, I could not make sense of their conversation.

"How many signs do they have?" I asked the abbot.

"As many as we have words," he said. "Man is a social creature. He wants to make himself understood. Take away one means of doing that, and he'll find another."

After that I did not try so hard to understand the signs. For the moment I was content to work on my books. After all, both I and the Abbot were working to make sure that our knowledge was preserved, and that our words reached those who had need of them, I in my way, and he in his.

My anger over my long and ridiculous search also cooled with time. At first I had focused my ire on the salvager I had met at Fort Morgan, since it was he who told me that books like the one I was seeking were written "for the enlightenment of mankind." And yet, even if the salvager had believed this, he had not believed it strongly enough to actually chase after the book, to the neglect of everything else. *That* mistake was on me.

Besides, I couldn't really disagree with what Sara the Afterling had said, when she told me that it was irrational to be angry at a tool for having limits.

I was reminded of this one September morning in 2254, when I went to visit Dina in Moñumin, where she still kept her little one-room library for children. I brought her presents from the sisters — liquorice roots, and a manuscript copy of a long fairy tale about four children and a talking lion and a portal to another world.

"You'll be glad," I said to Dina. "I've come with much better gifts than last time."

"Are you talking about the kitten book?" she said. And when I tried apologizing again for leaving her with something so useless, she just interrupted me, saying: "Oh, Mara, that's one of the children's favorites. The younger kids are always asking me to read it to them."

"Is it really?" I asked, almost in disbelief.

"Yes, it really is," said Dina. And then I considered telling her how much misery I had suffered on account of that book, but I decided not to, since she really seemed quite pleased with it.

Dina did not try to convince me that it was brilliant, or profound, or even just unique. To her it was enough that the children (or at least the younger children) liked it. But even this should not have surprised me as much as it did. Children like regularity. They like to be told the same story over and over. They do not demand originality. They are content with what is familiar and pleasant.

That, I supposed, must be why children like kaleidoscopes. There is no mind inside a kaleidoscope: the images that it makes do not tell you anything about the world, the way that a good painting does. After all, it is only a few bits of rotating glass, encased within mirrors, and transformed into a glittering pattern that goes on and on. The "thinking machine" might as well have been a kaleidoscope for words; it did not *tell* you anything, it only made a pretty pattern of language that went on and on.

But if you were not expecting it to do anything else, it really could not harm you.

And so, that afternoon, when the children gathered in the courtyard, and the question of "what shall I read first" was answered by cries of "Luna! Luna!" I sat with them and listened as Dina opened the book, turned its broad, colorful pages toward her listeners, and began to read:

"Once upon a time, in a small village nestled in the mountains, there lived a curious kitten named Luna...."

Cal Bannerman

Lights Out

I THINK WE WERE ALL a little disappointed with how things ended for the human race. There was nothing Hollywood about it. No explosions. No T-virus. A distinct lack of tsunamis, asteroids, solar flares. Gojira didn't make an appearance, neither did Thanos. Not one popular-culture reference fit the bill. Our unique flaw was a desire to frame the end of the world as perpetually impending. My jii-jii was a psychologist, and my baa-baa an anthropologist, so together I'm sure they could've explained why people did this. But I, well, I tell stories. I can give you only stray thoughts.

By my reckoning we conjured catastrophes because we desired something to aim for. The promise of a way out, should all go to hell anyway. The end of the line provided a tangible importance to our lives. Instead of counting ourselves as one among 9.8 billion successful sperm-egg combos — destined to live out a life of consumption, procreation, and hibernation — we brought into being a reason to exist: Armageddon.

It was written in the holy books before they went out of fashion, and subsequently in tabloid headlines. Blockbuster movies envisaged it in a hundred different scenarios, each set just a decade or two in the future. Novels and poetry imagined life post-apocalyptic; dystopias and utopias bereft and brimming with the resilience of the apex species. We humans were a global society of obsessive-compulsives, guzzling down Mayan calendars, millennium bugs, stock market crashes, global warming, atom bombs. When one passed and nothing changed we called it survival, not lunacy.

We were still casting stones of the apocalypse in our moving picture rooms, the faces of neurotically anxious children illuminated by the light from their pocket mirrors, when first it became apparent that the end of the human race was already underway.

Apparently, a news story ran about how the Afghan poppy farmers of Helmand province were experiencing a crop blight. The following week, NHK's Japanese-Afghan correspondent reported that it wasn't a blight, but a massive crop failure. Two months later and no farmer worth their plow could get seed to sprout. Moralists and policymakers celebrated (no more poppy meant no more H), whilst junkies and pharmaceutical boards got the sickness.

My grandparents told me that the failure of the poppy crop soon spread worldwide, with explanations as varied and colorful as the responses to it, but no real concrete evidence or theories either way. They also said that few people really took notice. Only later, when they were in their thirties and pregnant with my mum, when not just poppy but wheat, carrot, daikon, sweet potato, cotton, grape and coca were as extinct as the bumble-bee, did it dawn on Earth's dwindling population that somewhere down the generations humankind had taken a turn for the complacent.

According to the Others, Lights Out was a gradual, largely undramatic episode. They said that the last volt of grid electricity trembled through the last underground conductor to power the lamp by my mum's last bed, in a maternity ward the day I was born. Some of the Others called me by a name which meant *the first light of a new day*. They said I was blessed not to have known the old life, not to be able to mourn for it. But I think my father always disliked that name—my mother was part of that old life, and for the few years I knew my dad he was often sad about that. Sad or angry. Angry at the world. Angry at his parents' generation or grandparents' generation. Angry at me.

After dad left, the rest of Tokyo seemed to collapse under the weight of his absence, like maybe he'd been holding more than just memories on his pale, spindly shoulders.

And so I began telling stories. Hoping that if I remembered his world vividly enough, he might in some way rejoin mine. Hoping that if enough people shared my stories, together we might prop back up the brittle bones of our home. You see, we survivors love stories of the old world—even more than our own memories.

It seems odd, in a world where we must scavenge and hunt for our food—where at thirteen I enjoyed my last and only taste of tinned edamame, by then already years out of date—that stories should hold any currency.

Currency. My grandparents told me all about that concept, about money, before they died. They said that in their time the earth had overflowed with food. Food and music and transportation and space and technology and medicine. Healthy living, I guess you'd call it. Seems they had enough of everything that no one should have wanted for anything, except for this thing called money. Money, Jii-jii said, was a number you were assigned at birth. Apparently, if you were lucky, over time you could increase that number a couple of digits. Of course, then there were the pandemics, the earthquakes and wars, when almost everyone's number dropped (though I never really understood why). Anyway, though there were enough resources to go around, you could only actually enjoy them when your number got high enough, and for most people it never did.

Today, we don't have money. We take what we can and share it with whoever's left. But stories, well. If the gift of storytelling could be likened to money, then I guess you'd say my number's pretty high. In exchange for a good story—especially a story from before Lights Out—folk will give almost anything.

Life is slow, in what remains of Tokyo—a crumbling collection of monoliths most of us just call the Old Place.

For a long time, the Old Place has been a good place to call home. In the guts of the city—massive storage tanks beneath empty 7-Elevens, concealed vaults in the bellies of mansions, the subterranean levels of hospitals—we discovered reserves of fuel, food, medicines. Some of us found weapons stashed in evidence lock-ups or police armories which we used for hunting. In supermarkets and in restaurants were stores of canned goods, stacked alongside immeasurable liters of cooking oil, which at a push could power generators.

All said and done, the transition from Lights Out to the lives we lead now was at least smoother in the Old Place than it was for those stuck elsewhere.

To most survivors in the early years, nothing outside of petrol, oil, cans, and pills mattered much. But to me, the real treasures could be found where few cared to look. Refuse dumps, for one. Yumenoshima and Umi-no-mori—trash-heap islands in Tokyo bay—were the regular sites of my scavenger hunts. Beaches, too, and the banks of the Sumida often excited me more than, say, an overlooked storage cupboard in a grocery store.

I had my grandparents' tales, of course, but by the time I was old enough to really listen, their stories had become confused, half-remembered, all the way forgotten. The treasures I uncovered trawling the shores of places like Yumenoshima painted a fuller picture of life in the old world than their stories ever could have.

Among my finds—which I keep now in neat stacks and arrangements, like the Ancients used to keep their houses—are thousands of flimsy, translucent plastic hoops. Four to a set, arranged in a square. Jewelry, perhaps, or packaging, though I like to think they were once a crucial part of wedding rites—the couple symbolically joined at the wrist, bound in plastic.

Branded pocket mirrors are abundant, too, decorated with bitten-apples, embossed buttons, camera lenses, unrecognizable words like Samsung and Huawei. It seems there may once have been a way to power them: turn them "on." Just like most things from before. Whatever they were, though, it seems clear to me that the Ancients were captivated by their own reflection.

I find a lot of brightly colored figurines of harder plastic, too: anthropomorphic characters; metal men; slender, white-skinned dolls with blonde hair and blue eyes and no discernible genitalia. A lot of these odd idols wield weaponry, some of which is like that described in my jii-jii's stories of war; some resembling those we found in the police stations and army barracks; some entirely alien. Effigies, I imagine, or tokens meant to ward off the bloodlust they represented. Perhaps the stranger ones bear the likenesses of old-world gods, prayed to in hopes of salvation from invented cataclysms.

Of all of my finds, though, there is one which I covet more than the rest. Fujifilms.

They are extremely hard to come by. And no wonder. They're immeasurably precious, and almost impossible to describe without having seen one for yourself. On a rectangle of card about the size of a hand is printed on one side the word 'Fujifilm', and on the other, a picture. Curious, though not impossible, but here's the thing: with all of the garbage I've searched through there are always patterns, always recurrences. The plastic wedding bands, for example, are all alike. The totem figurines often part of a set. I even have several identical copies of the same illustrated book, predictions of an apocalypse called *Attack on Titan*.

But Fujifilms are different.

Every single one of them is different. Each picture totally and utterly unique, whether they share common traits or not. And get this, the glossy images are often of people. Ancient people. People in bars, restaurants, public parks. Hundreds of people intermingling on the busy streets of a fantastical Tokyo, crisp and clean and functioning. Healthy people. Happy people.

At first I took them to be paintings. Intensely realistic paintings, but paintings all the same. Only you can't wash these images off; you can't smudge or alter them as you might paint. There's no texture to the things, either. Fujis are exactly smooth. Like they were just made that way.

Then one day, whilst raiding an empty apartment block off Koishikawa marshes (formerly Koishikawa Botanical Gardens, if the fading signs are correct), I found a Fuji which changed everything.

Under the awnings of a whitewashed café, sat at a circular table shiny with metal, one shaven leg curled over the knee of the other, was a woman. From between two fingers of her right hand she dangled a thin white stick, about two inches long. I recognized it as a "cigarette," having found countless stubs of the things—their yellowed filters outliving the tobacco plant by many decades. In her left hand, the woman clutched a pocket mirror. She wore a wide, floppy hat, her eyes hidden behind a pair of heavy sunglasses, her face tilted slightly from the focal point of the image, perhaps shy.

And I recognized her.

She was my grandma. *My* baa-baa, only younger than I'd ever known her. Perhaps as young as I was in that moment. It was unmistakably her. Those were her wide cheekbones, her threadbare eyebrows. The way she held her cigarette the same as she used to finger kindling absentmindedly as we huddled round a fire. Without doubt, the blotched scarring on the woman's upper arm was the result of injuries baa-baa had sustained as a child at the mercy of a neighbor's dog.

In finding that Fujifilm I learned of their true value. They were not rendered images of an imagined world. They were moments. Real, genuine moments of history, captured by some old-word device; a reflection in a pocket mirror, perhaps, transferred to card by some forgotten trick.

Though my grandma was long gone, her face fading from memory with each passing year, now suddenly she had been returned to me. Preserved eternally in my hands.

I don't remember crying, but I do remember the exhaustion. The difficulty with which I finally dragged myself from that Bunkyo apartment hours later, having failed to find more memories, believing wholeheartedly that I could find a Fuji of my parents, if only I searched hard enough.

People come to me now from far and wide. They hear of the woman called *the first light of a new day*, the one who resides in the Old Place.

When they reach me, they don't know what to say. But I do. That's why they come, after all. And I begin, always, with a picture: a woman at a table, gentle smile on her lips: my baa-baa—at which they weep.

They ask how it could be possible that she is both there, in my hand, and gone from this earth. They want the same for themselves. They feel the way I felt as I crawled on hands and knees from the Koishikawa marshes, my world at once enlightened and shattered.

Together we look through my stack of Fujis collected over the years. We take time with each, as I relay the stories behind them. It doesn't matter if the tales are real, or not. Doesn't matter how close I am to the reality stored in those images. All that matters to my visitors is the reanimation of our history which my stories allow. That, and the hope that they, too, may find in my Fujis a certain someone; a long lost relative, friend, an acquaintance, anyone from before the darkness.

I remember one woman in particular, her back bent stiff, elbows grinding audibly as she stroked the faces which peered out at her, young and hopeful, from the faded cards.

She had traveled hundreds of miles on foot, from the mountain holdouts of Niigata Prefecture to the urban sprawl of Tokyo, just to taste the old world. And there, midway through the pile of memories, she found herself. Barely nineteen years old, face pressed against her wife-to-be (though, she told me, back then they had yet to uncover their love for each other).

I remember expecting the tears I'd seen in others, yet the old lady shed none. She only looked at me, bowed in thanks, smiled. She placed the Fuji face down atop the viewed pile, continued flicking through the others.

I remember telling her somewhat dumbfounded that the Fuji was hers. That she could keep it; that she should. She just laughed and shook her head.

"You keep it," she said, her voice a whisper. "Another story to tell." Then she took my hand, and though her eyes were cataract clouds somehow I knew how deeply she saw.

"They are always with us, you know; whether you can see them or not. It is a gift beyond any to see her face again, but she was always there." She gestured to the air, the concrete, the weeds growing around us. "Whoever it is you ache for, they are in everything you touch, everything you see, hear, breathe. You need only let them in."

I remember walking the old woman to the edges of the Old Place, beyond which grew jungle and wasteland. Her return journey north would be arduous and I wondered if she even hoped to make it.

I watched her go, admiring the stubbornness of her step; saw her stop and turn.

"Oh, and sweetheart?"

"Yes?"

"They're called photographs."

Anthony St. George

Navigating the Immortals

I SIGHED, re-reading the couplet I had just finished scratching into my bedroom wall.

Morning mists push through the bay, shrouding the peaks on high,
There, in all their glory, dance the Immortals of Penglai.

Now, leaving sixteen, I am an immortal. This is the story of my ascent.

"Tira," Captain Perez said, her blue eyes bright despite the misty winter light over San Francisco Bay. We were sitting in the fern-lush courtyard of our community convening place, the brutalist concrete fortress of the abandoned St. Stephen's church. It was one of the few Belvedere buildings that were still inhabitable. "Read the decision back to us."

Perez was my adoptive mother, but as the community scribe, I maintained a respectful formality with her in these meetings.

"By a vote of eighty-seven to two," I read my sign-scrawl on the tablet screen, "it is hereby resolved that the community will house itself on AngelTip."

"That's all well and good," a pointy-chinned woman called out from the gathered crowd of voters. "But how are we going to get there? It's not like we have any way to get on the island."

"And getting just a few of those houses isn't going to help all of us. Don't you think the 'Lords of AngelTip' will fight back?" one of our night watchfolk asked, using the local slang for any wealthy community.

Looking at Perez before jumping in, Captain Dy, my other parental figure, halted the dissenters. "We expect there'll be a tipping point, and once a few of us have moved in, they'll abandon the place quickly. Most of these houses are their second or third ones, and they're rarely or never there."

"Excuse me," an unfamiliar woman in her thirties piped up from the crowd. A thick head of wavy reddish-caramel hair framed her dark face. The hair was probably the work of CRISPR modifications, but you usually only saw that on wealthy people. No one in our community had the means for that. "I think I can help you."

Perez held up her hand. "Identify yourself."

"I live on AngelTip. If you want to get on our island, don't you think you might want some input on whether we'll take you?"

"Hold it, hold it," Dy chimed in. "You shouldn't be here. For all we know, you're an infiltrator." Meetings were open but unguarded. Non-flyers didn't tend to have much interest in our issues and organizing. Two men sitting near the woman started to rise to their feet, but Dy motioned them to stay put. "It's all right, guys," he said, "Let's just stay calm until we hear what she has to say. Agreed, Captain Perez?"

"Agreed. Identify yourself," she said.

"My name is Thelia Adayemi," the woman said, lifting her chest proudly. "I want to help."

Unsolicited help? What was this — a glimmer of hope?

Our flyer community had been camping in the mud at the north end of the bay for almost a year. We came from near and far: families flooded out of the flats of the East and South Bay; relatives who had made their way to the Bay Area from the storms and fighting in Houston and the water riots of Los Angeles and Phoenix; and even families from the Eastern Shore of Maryland, their homes collapsing into the waters of the Chesapeake Bay. Our community was officially registered with the Feds in Chicago as a small, self-formed flyer community: eighty-nine voting units but over four hundred and fifty mouths to feed and clothe. Our families were domiciled in the garages and front yards of Belvedere's raccoon-infested, condemned houses, with St. Stephen's serving as our central command and community kitchen.

"Why would you help us?" I asked. My first reaction to most strangers was usually suspicion these days. "You people live safe and in luxury. You don't want rabble like us."

"Your leader already explained it. So many people aren't living there even now. And those that do can afford to move. I can help persuade them ... and get you approval from Governor Corey."

The island community had self-assembled after Hayward Quake 2. Belvedere's original population of bankers, entrepreneurs, media moguls, and their flaneur descendants formed a consortium and bought out the former State Park of Angel Island as a bailout to the Bay Area Regional Authority. The payment had enabled a massive influx of funds for nine months of daily rations, tents, and sleepsacks for communities like ours. In exchange, the new owners were permitted to establish a well-defended refuge of ferrock dug-out homes with phenomenal views of the bay, only a ten-minute ride on a shooter, the two- and four-person aerial conveyances issued only to the Bay Guard, to the business end of San Francisco. *Was it a fair trade? At the time, the exhausted and starving amongst us thought so.*

I shook my head. It was too good to be true.

"Look, let's take a break," Perez addressed the crowd. "Strategy Committee, join us in the conference room."

Ten of us entered the meeting hall. Adayemi, clad simply in white painter's pants, an olive-green cashmere sweater, and navy cotton scarf, strode over to the table and pulled up a chair.

"Let me explain what I can do and why I want to. What are your other options? An old camp like Manzanar or one of the BrightFuture Communities?"

Hearing this, Perez looked around our group with raised eyebrows as if chastening an expected retort. Instead most of us looked down sheepishly, having argued over these and our other undesirable choices many times: the first was an infamous Japanese internment camp of the previous century located in Eastern California; the second, a series of tracts across the Lower Plains rumored to be built near electric vehicle battery dumping grounds.

As much as I immediately disliked her for her wealth, there was something appealing about Ms. Adayemi. Was it just that she was clean? Or that she looked like she could make anything come true? She was clearly better than what I'd grown up with, at least: my mother had been sent to prison for the attempted murder of her sister, and my father subsequently launched himself headfirst into melting gums and a meth-fentanyl overdose.

A memory came to me as Ms. Adayemi introduced her background. Dy, my former middle school math teacher, took me on when my father died. Perez, an out-of-work psychologist and friend of Dy's, invited us to join the camp, and together they co-parented me as best they could. I was grateful to them both. Their patience and understanding had stopped me from my early periodic fits of rage. Anger at my parents gnawed its way into my consciousness, bursting out whenever I was confronted by betrayal. I didn't have a lot of friends because my responses to conflict with them tended toward stabbing them with my pencil or giving them a bloody nose.

Dy had stopped me from my worst instincts numerous times. "You've got to be careful with that, Tira. If you don't control it, you'll end up where your mother did."

Perez would finish off the warning, "Always remember, Tira. Without a lot of work on yourself, you become one parent and marry the other."

I had my father's chestnut-brown hair and my mother's high cheekbones and long legs; that was plenty enough to inherit, and I vowed to keep it at that.

Ms. Adayemi's voice brought me back to the room. "Look, let's start slowly. Let one trustworthy family into one empty house I know I can get you into. You can't let anyone know I'm helping—no one else in your community and no one on AngelTip. Once you start, I can work with the governor to convince some of the AngelTip families to leave. They'll see some flyer families taking over my ex's place and get uncomfortable. There are some families that are already planning on moving to take up Federal administration positions in Chicago. Couple their dislike of flyers, maybe add in some incentive funding from the government for diehards, and we'll have the island cleared within six months."

I tried to make sense of her proposal in light of Dy's past explanations of how we'd gotten to where we were: two years prior, Chicago had been declared the capital of the Central States, the inheritor of all that DC had been unable to manage. The husk of a Federal government was trying to keep what was left of the United States together. Furious at the West Coast states' extortion of quasi-independence in exchange for access to its ports, the Feds tended to be erratic in choosing when and whom to help in a crisis. Those who could afford it were happy to leave the Bay Area for the segregation—or what they called "safety"—of Chicago's newly built walled defenses. This is where Ms. Adayemi saw the cracks in their walls of money.

The captains nodded, and the conversation continued until all in the room were convinced that her plan and contacts were more plausible than any non-plan they'd been poking at. With the report-out of Ms. Adayemi's idea back to the crowd in the courtyard, tight shoulders and stiff necks began to relax.

"Be it resolved," I read aloud to the committee of eighty-nine soon after the announcement, "that Ms. Adayemi may assist the community in negotiating the opening of island units. Her status is to remain confidential, and she retains no voting rights."

A three-hour Q&A session followed, Ms. Adayemi's residential, career, and family history thoroughly probed before a unanimous vote gave her the status of "Ally."

Renewed by this new sense of hope, families worked their connections and bartered to acquire conveyances—skiffs, motorboats, sailboats, even makeshift drum-barrel rafts. Evening storytime started up again, instilling excitement in the camp's children. Stories became increasingly optimistic. Save for those by a few detractors who were still convinced that we were on the wrong path.

"What's all this about the island being haunted?" one of the late-shift watch-folk asked at one storytime about a week later. I suspected that the skeptical woman from the first vote had started the rumor.

"What are you talking about? Don't be ridiculous. Haunted by what?" Perez glared at the woman, checking the faces of the kids sitting nearest the hearth fire for fear.

"By the ghosts of the Chinese immigrants. The ones held there for processing in the early twentieth century. Some say you can feel them if you run your hands over the poems they carved into the walls of the old buildings. Poems of longing for home."

"Those buildings are gone," Dy said, "Don't go scaring the children just because you don't want to live there. We should call it Penglai."

People looked around at each other in question.

Seeing the confusion, Dy, a Filipino of Chinese descent whose grandparents often dragged him to local performances of mythtellers and Chinese operas, clarified, "Penglai is the unreachable, mythical mountain island between China and Korea. It's said to be inhabited by eight deities. Let's just say we're going to go live on the Island of Immortals."

Some eyes rolled, but the eyes of most children grew wide.

From that evening, as the fog rolled in from the Golden Gate and the strings of shimmering fairy lights of the bunkers of conspicuous consumption began to glow, Dy would spend storytime telling enticing tales of the island's inhabitants: An island with a full water-table and cisterns, happy goats and chickens, immortals sitting down at their dinner tables with their children protected and warm, an island full of apple trees to fill bellies and heal the sick.

"Before the next rainy season," he said, "those warm homes and full bellies will be yours."

"You need to get to bed," Perez said.

It was eight P.M., three weeks after the start of "Operation Penglai," an hour before Perez and Dy usually sent me to bed.

"What have I done?" I asked. "This isn't fair!" They were so steadily kind and permissive that I quickly protested any deviation.

"Nothing," she said. "I have to get you up in the middle of the night. I need you to take a message to Ms. Adayemi." Communication with Ms. Adayemi had to be secretive and personal to reduce the risk that AngelTip residents would figure out her maneuvering.

At the unpleasant hour of four A.M., wrapped in two sweaters and a bark-brown poncho, I clambered into a rowboat that we'd commandeered from an unoccupied houseboat in Sausalito and rowed quietly to AngelTip.

Adayemi had told me where the guardhouses were around the island's perimeter, and I shot for a willow thicket under a steep bank unmarked by their intermittent searchlights. When I neared the steep shore, I grabbed some stalks to pull the boat close in, and Ms. Adayemi, who had been waiting for me, slipped into the waist-deep water to tie it up. Earlier that afternoon she had gotten word of where to land to Perez, who had guided me as she pushed me off from the opposite shore.

"Not a chance, ladies," an amplified male voice came from behind a flashlight glaring at us.

Adrenaline shot my hands up in surrender, but I remained quiet.

"What are you doing here at this hour? Thinking of scavenging?"

"Nightfishing," I said, lifting up some coils and hooks Dy had thrown in the boat as my cover.

"At this hour? You're lying. Get up here." A thick-gloved arm reached down through the bushes to help me onshore.

I froze, unsure whether to abort or at least get myself on the island and go from there.

"It's okay, young lady," a familiar voice came out from behind the man. "Let Tarkus help you up. I'll handle her."

With only a few scrapes from the branches, the man pulled me up, and I found myself in the glow of a candle lantern in front of Ms. Adayemi.

"What are you doing here at this hour, Ms. Adayemi?"

"Tarkus, this is no one's business, you understand? No one's ... and I've got a nice gift for your son, by the way," she added, her jaw set with determination.

"Yes, Ms. Adayemi."

She reached for my hand and whispered to me as she pulled me close, "Let him think what they want about you and me," she said, "No doubt he'll make up something salacious if I have to get him fired, but the neighbors will favor me over one of our contract workers."

I followed Ms. Adayemi barefoot up the cold, mist-moistened trail, dodging fallen acorns and scratchy pine twigs along the way. We passed low-roofed, hollow-dark caverns of houses as we ascended to her home. The needle-thin beams of red light passing from post to post indicated the pulse-laser defenses the wealthy used to protect their homes. "I've been monitoring these houses," Ms. Adayemi said. "Usually, houses with beams on more than a month means they're good targets for housing your lot. We leave the warning tracers on when we're away for any length of time so neighbors and the defense team don't get hurt. When we're home, we don't turn them on. They keep away any scavengers that may elude the guards."

"There must have been five of those fences already."

"At least seven," she corrected me. "And those homes are ready for your families to move in as soon as I make a few arrangements with Governor Corey."

Entering her gate, I noticed the solar panels and wind generators that powered her house, just like the others. "We keep ourselves sustainable, so we don't have to rely on anything off-island. We've got communal gardens. We pay some of the guards' kids to do the weeding."

Ms. Adayemi brought me into her front sitting room, the windows looking south at the earthquake-slanted towers of San Francisco, their searchlights scanning the bay for unapproved civilian activity around its shores.

We sat on a moss-colored, soft tweed couch, and I stretched out my feet to warm them by the fire.

In this delicious comfort, my suspicion at her kindness reared its head. "Why are you doing this?" I asked.

"Helping you all?" I took the mug of twig tea she offered me. Its steam smelled of the cheap bamboo tea they used to give us in primary school. "Well, because you deserve it. Any small bit I can do to ease suffering ... isn't that what we're here on this planet to do?"

"But you could just move like the rest of them. Take off to somewhere safer and avoid people like us."

"And lose this view? This beauty? This weather?" She smiled, a devil in her grin. "Not a chance. You can stay the night. I'll give you a message for Perez and Dy in the morning. You can have my bed."

After one last look at the view, she led me to her bedroom through corridors of art and hung costumery and left me there in thick-blanketed splendor. Within minutes, amidst softness I hadn't felt in, well, since ever, I fell asleep to the sound of the basso foghorn duet, two somber night owls protecting the bay.

After a sleep-in, Ms. Adayemi fed me three of her blue-shelled Araucana chickens' eggs from her garden, after which she let me explore her home and ponder the oil paintings and multi-media artwork on her walls. "They're a reminder of life before the Broken Wars," she said, referring to the various battles between states in their bid for secession, inclusion, or vengeance. She pointed out images in the depictions of life before the crumbling: the addiction to computers, the AI avatars, false relationships, false representations, waves of news to manipulate micro-populations to sway votes, the speed to violence. "Before then, there was a prevalence of fluffy white clouds and laughing children in public art. After the Big Mistake with China, there was a shift to blacks and browns and a return to the melting faces of post-World War I art."

I'd never been to a museum. Her explanations meant nothing to me.

Turning the corner into the hall, I came upon an unframed, chipped board that read:

雲霧潺潺也暗天，
蟲聲唧唧月微明。
悲苦相連天相遣，
愁人獨坐倚窗邊。

Below it was a translation on a laminated white card:

As the clouds and fog gather, the sky darkens.
With the chirps of crickets, a sliver of moon.
Sadness and bitterness come together, sent forth by heaven.
Anxious, sitting alone, I lean against the window.

"What is this?" I asked.

"Oh, that? Isn't that interesting? It's a piece of the wall rescued from the immigration hall down on the shore before the flooding started. The governor gave it to me as a memento when we gave them the funding to feed the flyers."

"When you bought this island . . ." I said, mostly to myself, unsure whether I wanted her to hear me. I changed my tone. "Is that describing you here?"

Ms. Adayemi laughed. "Me? No, of course not! The clouds and the moon, yes, I've seen that many times here. But sad? Here? Not that I ever remember."

She led me back through the living room. It wasn't just artwork that graced her home. As we walked through, she pointed out some of her favorite treasures: her contraband, black-and-gold Indonesian batik runner; her table made by an Argentinian designer banned from entry into the U.S. in a pointless political tit-for-tat; a collection of salvaged hand-sewn, sun-bleached children's dolls from the Appalachian rebel counties.

"How'd you get all this?" I asked.

"Well, I worked hard." Out over the bay, drone messengers, shooters, and patrol boats periodically shot by in their fly lanes. A multiplicity of colors denoted their classification as delivery, defense, or transportation.

"You worked?"

"Yes, indeed," she said, her eyes drifting up into a memory. "To be fair, I did start off with a leg up. I had a great uncle who moved from Nigeria to Mali, where he made a fortune developing the Sahara hyperloops." I recognized the term: the underground north-south and east-west bullet trains crossing under the massive desert. In our community schooling, Perez had drilled into our heads how communities succeed with united, concerted effort, and this was an example of how multi-nation investment had helped launch the economic rocket-ship of the Union of Sub-Saharan Africa. "My profligate parents made sure we never saw any of that money," said Adayemi. "Thankfully, my grandmother took me from them and made sure I was educated in remediation law, which she saw as an underdeveloped field. She got us to Switzerland, where I studied hard to make something of myself. I would have stayed there if not for falling in love with the Bay Area on a business trip."

"You left Switzerland for this?"

"It was before the cataclysms. I could go back to Switzerland, I guess. But I can build my world better here."

"Why are you helping us here?"

"Well, maybe it's because of you."

I froze for a second, and she saw it. Was this some kind of pass at me? I stepped back from the edge of where my nerve endings were firing.

"I mean, I see someone young like you and know you deserve more. You and your friends should have the chances I had. I feel like I can do something here. The older people will cope regardless of what I do, but young people like you need to get some stability so that you can be a force in the world."

"I'm a force." This was a mantra we had been taught to repeat in primary school. I followed up with my own uncertainty. "I mean, I do my piece."

"Yes, you're a scribe, but I see that you can do more."

"You'll teach me?" I asked.

"Once the island is settled, and we're all together. Of course." She patted my shoulder. "Oh wait, first comes the party season. Then we can start."

There it was. While part of me was thrilled at this attention, this last statement threw me. *Party season? Why were parties important? And why did they take precedence over teaching me?*

Seeing the doubt on my face, she quickly clarified. "I mean, a lot of how I get what we need is through parties. More important than your school learning is who your friends are. That can be your first lesson."

I recoiled at the shallowness of the idea. Or maybe it was the idea of having and keeping friends.

We didn't see much of Ms. Adayemi over the next two weeks. Perez kept up with my tutelage in information system structures—a euphemism for basic hacking skills. Dy taught me the way around an illegal, carbon-fuel-run outboard motor. "These skills will get you farther than anything Ms. Adayemi can teach you." The infotech skills weren't illegal. They were what every pre-teen and high-schooler was taught in official public schools. It's just that savvy flyer communities realized that to get things done, sometimes you need to turn those essential skills into something more intrusive.

"How's your learning going, by the way? What has Ms. Adayemi been teaching you?"

"I've been memorizing the names of the governor's connections."

"That sounds odd. What for?"

"Ms. Adayemi wants me to memorize the personal networks so that I can learn how re-developers and corporations pull strings to get things like increased security from the Bay Guard, faster equipment delivery, or food for their workers." Ms. Adayemi insisted this, coupled with reading the gossip comms on local philanthropists, would be the foundation of my future success under her tutelage. I swallowed my disdain for the concept but committed names to memory in case my instincts were wrong.

As the last rains of winter spilled into the windy days of spring, Dy made an announcement. "The conveyances have been requisitioned, and most of the houses are ready." Dy's face glowed with a mix of pride, relief, and defiance.

We were transferring on Memorial Day, thinking any of the island's remaining wealthy would be away starting their summer, and the Bay Guard would be tied up with parades and demonstrations around the bay. We began to offload at dawn, but within a half-hour of tying up, two Bay Guard PT boats pushed in through the semicircle of our boats approaching the docks. The bark of a kevlar-clad commandant came over the comms on all boats. "Scavenger worms relent! Who's responsible here? Reveal yourself right now!"

"Society's to blame!" Boat captains jammed the officer's comms device with the popular refrain of the time.

"You are entering private land! You will be terminated if you do not retreat!" the commandant yelled back.

Dy, on the dock helping settlers with their transfer, responded. "The houses we will inhabit have been abandoned. We have a right to claim them."

"This is impossible. We have our orders. We have permission to exact retribution for illegal activity."

Perez and Dy looked at each other. Then Perez spat out, "You mean you want your bribe."

Before the officer could respond, a bolt of searing light sizzled into the water in front of one of the PT Boats. Over the comms, Ms. Adayemi's voice snarled, "Retribute this!"

Shocked eyes looked towards the island's peak where the shot had come from. "What the...!" the officer exclaimed. "You know that's not going to do you any good in the end, right? We've got forces we could drop onto the whole island. You'd be evicted by nightfall."

Perez responded, "This transfer is peaceful. The inhabitants have approved. We are not worth your time... You've got enough to do from the Gate to the Delta without bothering us." She motioned toward the bay with a flick of her head. "Stick to protecting your precious Alcatraz," she said. I looked at Dy, remembering his tales of pirate attempts to blow up the city's quantum-blockchain surveillance servers there.

"Tell your people to leave peacefully, and we'll forget all about it," the officer replied.

Ms. Adayemi's voice, now soft, floated in. "Commandant Irwin, I'm an owner and original resident here. I'm calling your Commander Thayer. Let me speak with him before things get out of hand."

Within minutes the Bay Guard boats were reversing away from the island, their engines soon drowned out by the enthusiastic burble and cheers of the families onshore.

After moving into our new unit, I was sent by Perez and Dy to ask Ms. Adayemi where the pulse blast had come from. "She'd never told us about weapons on the island," Perez said. "How'd they get such a thing? And how do we get trained on it? You know her best. You go find out."

Late that afternoon, after helping families settle in, I made my way up to the top of the island. Ms. Adayemi greeted me at her gate with an embrace, which should have felt welcoming but, to me, was more like forced intimacy.

After we'd settled on her sofa, I asked her about the morning. "What was that blast? How did you get permission for something like that?"

"Well," she said, her grin both mischievous and embarrassed. "It's a bit of a jerry-rigged device that I had Tarkus work out for me. It was the first time I'd tried it."

"What is it?"

"We'd always wanted a last-ditch defense for the island but could never get permission. Tarkus told me that by combining the energy sources of the fencing systems of the neighboring homes, I could create a pulse beam to put a hole in most anything, a boat, a drone, a shooter. It takes time to re-charge, but I figured one warning shot would get the point across."

"Isn't it going to get confiscated now?"

"It can be disassembled quickly. They wouldn't find anything."

"What do you mean?"

"The repeaters are disguised to look like sound systems for my parties. That and a few mirrors from my living room that I attach to the sun umbrella poles.

Here, I'll show you."

She got up from the sofa and took me around to the mirrors on the walls of her living and dining rooms and then pointed out slightly modified umbrella stands on her deck. She showed me how the stands held the mirrors and could capture the beams from the back fence of her property. The repeaters were disguised as stereo and karaoke equipment. It was a little involved with switches and equipment but not overly complicated, and easily dismantled.

"Can you teach me?" I asked.

Ms. Adayemi paused for a second before acquiescing. "It doesn't hurt to have a back-up. You're a good girl. Can I trust you not to get us in trouble?"

"I promise," I said.

Looking at me, Ms. Adayemi shook her head wistfully and said, "You're incredible. I see your strength, gentle but fierce. I wish I had a tenth of what you have. I can be too aggressive sometimes." She had briefly placed her hand on my shoulder and removed it to cover her heart. "But I guess you don't get what I have without it."

I looked around her living room at the candles on her dining table: the loftiest of the fairy lights of Penglai. "I'm teaching you how to win in this world. We'll get you over there ..." she thrust her chin towards the blue lights of the Governor's Welcome Hall on Twin Peaks above the hum of San Francisco. "We'll have you running this whole bay someday."

I looked around and forced a smile, thinking gratitude, feigning excitement, suddenly ready to leave. Why would I want to run the bay? It was enough to be with Perez and Dy, enough to gather with the families for group dinners, enough to practice my scribing skills and make my way into the working world across Route 101 in a year or two to be an admin assistant at one of the canning factories.

A dry "Thanks" was the best I could muster.

"But I got the Bay Guard off your back!" Ms. Adayemi's voice clanged around her courtyard. "We're all on good terms now."

Two months had passed, and the abandoned houses now housed ninety percent of our community. The remaining ten percent had been bought out by Governor Corey on behalf of the community. He got credit with the Feds for settling an independent community, a feather in his cap he could use for future negotiations and his subsequent election campaign. To convince the owners, he paid to move the island's remaining original inhabitants to safe communities in allied British Columbia.

"You've got to be kidding me," Dy said. "There's no way!"

"After all I've done for you?"

The knives in their voices began to reach my heart.

"C'mon, Dy," I said, unsure why I was taking her side.

"Yes, Tira?" He said, meaning, "Don't butt in."

"Dy, surely you told her. Don't tell me you and Perez have gone back on your deal?"

"There was no deal. Don't lie to save face." Dy looked at me with a stern eye, still not wanting me there.

"It's you who changed the terms!" Perez chimed in, raising her voice. "You said you would help clear the island. Your job was to encourage people to leave."

"Which I've done."

"But not in exchange for giving you the three top properties on the island!"

"Well, I should get something for my efforts." Her skin was wrinkle-free and glistening, her hair radiant.

"What are you going to do with three properties? You're putting out at least four families doing that."

"Think of it as a commission."

"This is not a bargaining world, Ms. Adayemi." Dy lifted his head and thrust back his shoulders. "You know we could make your life hell."

"Are you threatening me? I could just as easily get the Bay Guard back … if you like. Or there's always the pulse beam."

"You're threatening us now?"

I started to feel sick to my stomach. I had to stop the stalemate. "Ms. Adayemi, could you explain why? What do you intend to do with the property? Perhaps you were going to build a school?" I wanted to give her an out.

She looked at me with an impatient eye. "I don't have to explain. Maybe it's because I have a family of my own that I want to bring here."

"But you don't," slipped from my mouth. She'd never mentioned any other family, and there weren't pictures of a mate or any children that I'd seen.

"Friends, then. I want to feel safe."

"You're the safest person here!" Perez said. "Everyone here is grateful to you for your help. They bring you meals when you can't get off the island. They stand guard outside your place when the Bay Guard patrols the channel."

"What about the people you could continue to help?" I couldn't hold back.

"I've done my bit. Just give me what I want."

"Was this all just a way for you to get a compound that you don't need?" Dy asked.

"Don't need? Of course, I need it. The party season is just five months away."

The three of us looked at her dumbfounded.

"You need the places for parties?"

Ms. Adayemi looked at me, then back at Perez, "Ask Tira. She knows what I've taught her. She can start to put what I've taught her to work."

"Is that what you want, Tira?" Perez asked.

I held my tongue. This twist had thrown me. It was one thing to study to become an immortal, another to see that impulsiveness and sleight of hand were part of the practice.

"Look, if it helps sweeten the deal," Ms. Adayemi said to Perez, "I can hire some of your people as property managers and waitstaff. Don't you think some people would like some work on the island instead of having to head out in search of work every day?"

"What, five flyers, maybe ten, would get some intermittent work? That's hardly helpful," Dy said.

"Take it or leave it," she said. "I've done my bit. I'm flying in my designer and contractor in a few days."

"A contractor? Those homes are already empty? When did that happen?"

"I worked it out with Corey and convinced the families over the past few days. They'll leave in the next week after they sell some of their artwork. And I'm going to go on a brief vacation tonight, but don't get any ideas. My pulse beams will be on."

My eyes began to sting as the first cracks of a sinkhole formed in my stomach. Dy looked at me and saw one of my rages forming. "Tira, go take a walk. This decision doesn't concern you."

"Wait, Tira," Ms. Adayemi said to my back. I turned to meet her gaze. "I'm sorry this is such a surprise, but you wouldn't have agreed if I'd told you sooner." She held out her arm as if beckoning me back. "I see so much of me in you. I'll take care of you once I get back. I've already booked the shooter and backing out of that would cost too much."

Now she was getting thrifty? The cost had to be a drop in the bucket against what she must have spent already helping us.

"You know it only takes a few handheld mirrors for anyone to get past those beams, right?" I shot back at her. "And you taught me how to use the pulse beam. Who's to stop us mistaking your returning shooter for an intruder?"

"Oh ho! A threat, Tira? Yes, you need that fighting spirit. But this was not the time to reveal your hand."

"Tira!" Dy and Perez exclaimed in unison. "Get out of here. We'll handle this."

I stamped to the gate and would have slammed it if it hadn't opened and shut for me automatically.

I broke into a run and took a path that circumambulated the island. Were Dy and Perez going to let her get away with this? They weren't weak. They'd gotten all of us onto the island. Weakness didn't succeed like that. But how could they let this go? Wasn't I the one to stop her? Knock her out of the sky, and we'd be free of her machinations?

Or was that going to have me end up like my mother?

Then the third way occurred to me: Dy and Perez would take it to a community vote. She couldn't buy that vote. We had been through too much together for a few dollars to crack us. Anyone caught would be ostracized right off the island.

But maybe they'd vote to allow. Ms. Adayemi had done a lot for us. She did a lot for the clean-up of the bay. Wasn't she a good person? Wasn't she helping me? But did that mean I'd have to become devious too? What kind of a mentor was this and why weren't Dy and Perez more upset?

I circled the island three times before returning to our headquarters unit at the pier. Dy and Perez were there.

"I know how it's going to go," I said. "We'll take it to a vote, won't we?"

They nodded calmly and opened their arms to me.

"It's not supposed to be like this, is it?" I asked.

Shaking his head and then looking at Perez, Dy answered me. "Yes, Tira, this is how things work at the top. We've arrived. Welcome to the Island of the Immortals."

R. Jean Mathieu

Glâcehouse

When Mackenzie embarked Marie-Pier Corriveau's ancient Prius after winter finals, the muggy slurry of rain had been falling on Montréal for two weeks. A *Presse* headline bubbled up in her Google-vision that it was officially the heaviest since the 2045 tipping point, and recommended some journalistic debate on whether this meant climate change was plateauing. She waved it away as if it were one of the malarial mosquitos that had plagued Quebec since she'd enrolled at McGill. Finals were *over*, and she didn't have to worry about risks of the Quebec City dikes failing and flooding the Plains of Abraham, or persistent malaria outbreaks in Three Rivers, or threats to the wine grapes in what remained of the Gaspé peninsula.

"*Bonjour*-hi!" she chirped, clapping the passenger door shut. Marie-Pier replied in kind. "What's with the blue-and-white bumper sticker?"

"Protective camouflage." Marie-Pier's French accent was the carefully precise and internationalized sort favored by Quebec's more cosmopolitan classes. "We are going upriver to the heart of the Republic."

"Ew." Mackenzie scrunched her nose. "The *one* place on Earth where the maple leaf on my backpack doesn't help. You could have told me."

Marie-Pier clicked the ancient Prius into drive.

"I promised you snow," she replied. Then she reached into her history major's bag of seemingly endless old *souverainiste* folk songs, warbling: "My country, it isn't a country, it's *hiver*."

Winter.

The wipers swept the muggy rain from the windshield, and Marie-Pier pulled into the outbound traffic.

Their network died not long after Marie-Pier gassed up for the last time, in Sanguenay. The locals had regarded the Haitian heritage on her skin with suspicion until she addressed them in their impenetrable French thicker than dike walls. Then they reserved the Gross Eyes for Mackenzie's halting French that smacked of the textbook and the red maple leaf on her pack.

The English had faded away slowly, still omnipresent except on the signs back in Quebec City, then still babbling in the Googlesphere along through the rolling hills of the RQ-175 with their brittle post-tipping-point steppe grasses. She heard it on snowbird tongues at the rest stops and as a language option on the vending machines. But in Sanguenay, it elicited only blank stares or worse. Mackenzie wondered what it would be like in Péribonka, at the glâcehouse.

She'd read about the glâcehouses in her Ecological Engineering courses, whole enclosed microclimates and ecosystems under the cooling mirror-glass. The Republic of Quebec had poured billions into the most extensive and advanced glâcehouse network in the world, almost since independence, and could boast the largest stand of maples south of the fiftieth parallel for their trouble. When Mackenzie had innocently mentioned to Marie-Pier that, Alberta-born-and-bred, she had never seen snow, she'd been ecstatic at the prospect of an adventure with the Princess Royal of the McGill history department. Now ...

"Nervous?" Marie-Pier asked, bursting Mackenzie from her reverie. "*Ouais*, it's bizarre the first time out of network. Don't worry, there is network in Péribonka. Until then, we can trade stories, if you please."

"Sure!" Mackenzie's voice cracked. "Sounds great. You go first."

Marie-Pier parted her chapsticked lips.

"... just not one of your papers about neosocialist decentralization policy, okay?"

Marie-Pier's laugh was deep and sincere and unaffected. She was a very sweet person, once you got past the studied chilliness.

"That is a reason I like you, Mec," Marie-Pier said. "You know how to make me laugh. *D'accord, je raconte une autre...*"

Having codeswitched into French, she continued in that tongue:

"There's a story brought from *la Finis-terre* to *la Fin du Monde* on the other coast of the Atlantic. It tells a little like this:

There was a time before Paris, when a splendid city carved itself into the Atlantic, past the rocks of Brittany. They called it the City of Ys, *Ker-Ys* in the Breton tongue, and the Celtish king Gradlon ruled it. He inspired you English for your King Arthur, isn't that so."

"Pardon me, I'm *not* English, I am Albertan."

"You cried at Queen-Mother Kate's funeral, you're English." Marie-Pier smiled. She switched back: "She was a beautiful, shining city, her land reclaimed from the white waters of the Channel, the sea kept out by great locks which only

Gradlon could open, with the key around his neck. For a time, she was good, but soon her glory rotted to debauchery, and one night, someone took the key and opened the locks, flooding the city beneath the Atlantic waves. Some people, they tell it was Gradlon, which is unjust to me. Some tell of his daughter Dahut, the fallen woman, whom Gradlon threw from his horse into the hungry waters as he fled. Some tell it was the Devil himself, because he is everywhere in these stories."

She switched to the English: "But always there is a king, a key, a city, and the sea."

"Atlantis," Mackenzie replied. "The Deluge. A story in every culture."

"*Goddamn* on Atlantis!" Marie-Pier said, with unusual force. "They do not tell this story in English, or Polish or Chinese. They only tell it in French."

"And Breton."

"Yes, and Breton." Marie-Pier smiled at being corrected, her usual savoir-faire falling back into place.

"Did you tell me a climate change story by intent?" Mackenzie asked.

"But no. It is only on my mind. And you? What is your tale?"

As Mackenzie opened her mouth to tell a Zen story from her childhood sangha, the vision beyond the windshield took her breath away. The lukewarm water of Lac St.-Jean, sharp and blue as the skies overhead, lapped at the grassy shore. The Québécois village of Péribonka huddled by the shore picturesquely, no building daring to rise above the two-hundred-year-old church spire.

But next to the village, crouched over the old Point-Taillon Nature Reserve just across the river, the glâcehouse loomed. At this time of year, each panel was sealed tight, reflective as an ice sheet, so shining white that Mackenzie's eyes watered in the climate-controlled Prius cab. It resembled nothing so much as a glacier, an impossibly regular and unmistakably handmade glacier, white and blue as the Quebec flag that fluttered at its summit and so massive as to make mere mortals think of some earlier age of titans and giants.

"Voilà, Point-Taillon Glâcehouse," said Marie-Pier. She sounded bored. "The lake may no longer freeze and the hills may no longer know snow, but I promise you that, in there? in *there*, there is snow!"

Excitement had crept back into her voice, along with the Sanguenayan French. She sped down the road, ignoring Mackenzie's stunned wonder in favor of anticipating the precious powder. Mackenzie found herself burbling about the technological marvels that made the glâcehouses possible, the super-reflective mirror-glass material that each geodesic panel was made from, the passive-solar technology that cooled acres and acres underneath the polarized panels, their key role in preserving fragile ecosystems in the face of global temperature rise. Marie-Pier listened politely.

They parked on the town side of the Péribonka River, carrying Marie-Pier's five bags between them over the little bridge into a sunny plaza squeezed between the lapping water of the lake and the imposing immensity of the glâcehouse.

Mackenzie smiled to herself as she mentally catalogued various native plants in the plaza. Well, "native." Mackenzie recognized two mustard varietals from the southeastern United States. However, with the titanic shifts in Canadian climates *de nos jours*, Mackenzie mused that the likes of broomsedge, bee balm, and jessamine counted as "native" for a sweltering wet Quebec winter.

Before them, the glâcehouse was less a building than a natural feature, as far beyond human contrivance as the Saint Lawrence Seaway or the Canadian Shield. The sign above the enviro-lock loomed almost as large. Next to the interlaced blue-and-white sphere of the Glâcehouse project it bore the legend "MAISON DE GLÂCE DE POINT-TAILLON" and listed its credentials as part of the *ministère écologique de la République* and assured the *citoyens* of Québec that their tax dollars were well spent here.

Nowhere on the vast sign did Mackenzie see a single word of English. Even in Sanguenay, shrunk to near-illegibility and buried at the bottom of the signs, there'd been an English translation. Not here.

"Allons-y, Mec." Marie-Pier smiled. "Come on!"

They swept, with Québécois snowbirds and half of Péribonka, into a climate lock the size of their sorority house back at McGill. Mackenzie had been expecting the closet-sized climate locks they had in the Montréal Biospheres, or something like the switch-locks for traffic heading off-island. She certainly wasn't expecting a hall so vast it had its own concession where bored teenagers were selling coffee, poutine, and beer.

Finally, on the piped-in chime of church bells, the internal lock opened, and Mackenzie got her first glimpse inside a real glâcehouse. It took her frozen breath away.

It really was a *pays d'hiver*, a kingdom of winter!

Beneath the polarized sky the color of granite and the bright, fragile haze of the indoor cloud cover, the landscape was impossibly crisp and clear. The snow glittered like a billion diamonds from the rolling ground and from the huddled cluster of steep roofs near the lock and from the bare branches of maples — real sugar maples! — *Acer saccharum*, not like the sapless warm-weather maples outside.

As Mackenzie staggered behind the sophisticated strides of Marie-Pier, she truly felt winter for the first time. Jack Frost did not so much nip her nose as stride up and mug her. Her skin felt brittle and dry, buffeted by chills and simultaneously numbed to them. She gave an involuntary shudder, her body no longer her own to control, possessed by the sub-arctic iciness in the air.

"Your friend will freeze," someone noted in an arch baritone, "if she doesn't don something over her *T-shirt*."

All had been in French, except for the last word, which was twisted with such venom Mackenzie might have needed rubber gloves to handle it.

"It's not a T-shirt, my father, it is a hockey sweater," Marie-Pier replied.

Mackenzie spun on her heel, the cold forgotten in her surprise. The man before her towered like a giant, with crisp black curls behind a high, sharp, "purewool" widow's peak. His beard was the steely gray of the dome, shot through with shocks of snow white. Frost clung to the edges of that thick, well-kept beard. He'd swaddled his bulk in a padded greatcoat that gave him the proportions of Jos Montferrand. His sharp brown eyes were fixed on Mackenzie, the twitching wrinkles at the side of his nose suspended on the edge of a proper Gallic sneer.

This was Marie-Pier's father? What was he *doing* here?

"Forgive an old traditionalist," he said, in the same carefully international French as his daughter, "but I thought that sweaters were supposed to protect from the cold?"

"It is her first time in the snow." Marie-Pier's clipped tones were as brittle and cold as the air.

"Let me lend her my coat, then." He reached for the button at his throat, hidden as it was under a thick layer of vat-grown fur. "It is made for a proper winter."

"Th-thank you." Mackenzie's teeth chattered. She added: "*Merci.*"

At the sound of English, the great man's gloved fingers stopped. The stillness stretching out, each moment more and more of a dismissal of the tiny Anglo-Canadian in his little kingdom.

"But no." Marie-Pier interjected. "I will lend her one of the articles I brought myself. I have not forgotten how to live in winter. *Je me souviens.*"

I remember. The Québécois motto.

Her father paused and nodded.

"Did you also remember your vitamin D capsules?"

"But of course. Thank you for your concern."

"It's not often my daughter comes in out of the summer sun anymore," he grumbled.

"This is Mackenzie Moore," Marie-Pier said, as though she hadn't heard. "She studies ecology at McGill. She came to Montréal all the way from Alberta to study the glâcehouses and the ecologies you protect. She has never seen snow, so I brought her to share the country of winter with her."

Her father gave a Gallic shrug.

"Doctor Corriveau!" called a voice. "We've finished the Sector 23 soil analysis."

"Thank you, Corentin," replied Marie-Pier's father. He studied to the two coeds.

"Mess is in the *grande cabane* at eighteen hours. If it's not too cold for you."

With that, he turned on his heel and headed for one of the dark buildings crouched under its helmet of snow. Marie-Pier was already digging through one of her bags.

"Et *voilà*," said Marie-Pier, helping Mackenzie into a thick down coat. "I should have known that Annika Fatimah sweater was too thin for freezing temperatures."

"Doctor Corriveau …" Mackenzie breathed, her mind whirling.

Marie-Pier stiffened. "Yes?"

"Doctor Jean-Baptiste Corriveau?"

"Yes." Now her voice was resigned.

"He's your *father?!*"

"But yes." Marie-Pier said. She rattled off the answers to all the questions on Mackenzie's tongue: "I am the only begotten daughter of the grand Jean-Baptiste Corriveau. I spent most of my teenage years under this dome, before I came to university. That's why I know a little more about ecological engineering than the average history undergrad. And how did you *think* I got us overnighting berths under the glass?"

Honestly, she hadn't thought to ask. She hadn't thought of a lot of things, apparently.

"But he's a *jerk!*" Mackenzie's cold-numbed brain had finally caught up with her.

"Yes. He really, really is." Marie-Pier agreed. "And we're having supper with him. But first, let's claim our berths and drop off our bags. And get you into proper winter equipage."

Dr. Corriveau didn't want to eat with Mackenzie. Marie-Pier didn't want to eat with her father, but insisted on Mackenzie's presence as her terms of engagement. Mackenzie was torn between wanting to pick the brilliant man's brain and wanting to keep as far away as possible.

So, here they were, sitting at the captain's table, with the covert eyes of the couple dozen scientists who overwintered under the glâce sneaking looks at them all.

After a meek compliment on the pale yellow *soupe aux pois* (resulting in a short, smug lecture on Québec's cheese diversity), Mackenzie lapsed into silence as the French swirled around her. To her amazement, she could generally follow the gist of the conversation, and when she couldn't, Marie-Pier seemed to have a sixth sense for when to drop a hushed translation in English.

Dr. Corriveau was saying, "… the sugar maples have retreated farther north this year, just a lot of dying mass to feed controlled burns."

"It must be difficult for them." Marie-Pier noted. "Trees do not, as a rule, run very fast."

The old man huffed.

"As we learned on Gaspé," he said, "Québécois and animals can outrun the damned neverending summer, but trees and buildings can't. They only sink into the sea on their rotten earth."

Marie-Pier finished translating and turned toward her father.

"But it is not so easy out there, even in Péribonka. When was the last time Lac St.-Jean froze? The winter when I was fourteen?"

"Exactly, my girl." Dr. Corriveau nodded. "Every year, the December temperatures are a little warmer. It is why the glâcehouses are so important, keeping a little winter, the old hard winter, under glass ..."

"My father, you sermonize to two choirgirls." Marie-Pier gave that polite, political laugh she was practicing for when she ran for Présidente.

Her father continued, unimpeded.

"It worries me. Think of the plaza in front. We started with red maples and bloodroot, better suited for long summers. Then the mayapple crept up from New England and even the red maples withered, no matter how fast we spliced wet-winter genes in. Then it was milkweeds, and now it is mustards from shores and banks where French was never spoken. *Here*, on the Lac St.-Jean, in the heart of Québec!"

"Excuse me, the burning heart." Marie-Pier said. Zen-raised Mackenzie blinked in confusion, until Marie-Pier whispered to her "don't worry, it is only Québécois blaspheming." Mackenzie nodded. That was normal enough, at least.

"It is almost worse now than under confederation. You can pass laws against the English; you cannot pass laws against their weeds." Dr. Corriveau shook his head. "It is not so safe inside either. There have been failures, failures of people."

Dr. Corriveau did not look in Mackenzie's direction, making her target status painfully clear. Instead, he stared at his daughter's impassive face. "Do you remember your mother's operations passkeys? We named the OS after you?"

"*Je me souviens*," she carefully enunciated.

Dr. Corriveau's chuckle came from deep in his chest.

"When I said you take after your mother, I never meant your melanin. You've always been sharp. I've taken to keeping the master passkeys around my neck, next to my heart. A rosary, if our glâcehouse is a nave."

As Marie-Pier caught Mackenzie up on their conversation, an aide ran up to the table with a tablet. Dr. Corriveau chatted with him, thumbing the tablet and ignoring his daughter even as he talked over her.

"... like an endless *summer*" — in Dr. Corriveau's mouth, it sounded halfway between *Sumeria* and a curse — "fetid and unhealthy ..."

"But it is much cooler in Montréal." Mackenzie interjected, to stunned silence.

Even the aide paused. "The climate there is both more cooler and more … more stabilize than here. I think it is a microclimate issue, perhaps the lake, its, uh, how do you say *refraction index*?"

Dr. Corriveau told her. It was the first time he had spoken directly to her all night.

"*Merci beaucoup, M. le Professeur.*" Mackenzie had never gone wrong being *too* polite in French. "There are complex affairs, but of course. You know better as me. Climate change is real, and it melts snows and kills living things. But it is here much worse."

"Ah! 'But where are the snows of yesteryear?' " Dr. Corriveau quoted. Even Mackenzie smiled. François Villon, at least, she knew. "Thus it is even more imperative to preserve the snows here."

He turned to his daughter. "Speaking of, your blonde, she is impertinent."

Mackenzie turned red and hunkered down into her soup. Marie-Pier covered her by asking how Dr. Gauthier and his seabirds at the Île-Bonaventure glâcehouse were coming.

After dinner, Marie-Pier hooked her dark, dainty hand in the crook of Mackenzie's elbow and "suggested" an after-dinner constitutional. Mackenzie was in no mood to argue after a dinner in the French fashion, lasting hours. Soon, they were walking along the inside edge of the glâce paneling, the snow crunching under their feet and the cold prickling their cheeks, Mackenzie staring agape at her iridescent image in the glâce and burbling excited exclamations about the elegance of the technology.

"Mec, I didn't bring you up here for you to stare at yourself in the glâces!" Marie-Pier finally burst.

Mackenzie choked off her burbling. The father might have been white as snow and the daughter dark as maple, but they had the same proud hauteur and could wield it like a whip. She could *hear* the family resemblance.

"… I apologize, excuse me." Marie-Pier finally said, in much softer, cooler voice.

"It's hard seeing your father again," Mackenzie said.

"But yes," Marie-Pier replied, "we do not necessarily see eye-to-eye on everything. He thought you were my blonde!"

Mackenzie deadpanned: "But I'm a brunette."

The old joke brought tired smiles to both their faces.

"So … why *did* you bring me?" she hazarded.

"Because I am my father's daughter."

"Pardon?"

Marie-Pier laid a hand on Mackenzie's shoulder, and rotated her inward, toward the frozen heart of the glâcehouse.

"My father mentioned the last time the lake froze, when I was fourteen." Marie-Pier's breath shivered in the wintry air. "Some things, he forgot. I remember watching spellbound as the snow fell gently from the sky, like millions of millions of dandelion seeds all falling to earth. I remember lacing up my skates, and my ass freezing numb after I fell on the lake too many times. I remember throwing snowballs at all the Saint-Monique kids, laughing and screaming ourselves hoarse. I remember making maple taffy out the back and drinking my first coffee next to a warm wood fire. I felt like one of Father's *voyageur* heroes. It was magic."

She took a deep breath, as if she would inhale all of winter.

"The snow used to come every year, falling alike on the just and the unjust, on the Québécois and the English. Father is proud of his little 'country of winter.' Well, I am, too. But I think you deserve to see it same as I. I try not to let my pride rule me."

Mackenzie smiled. "You prefer to let your pride about your GPA and your delusions of grandeur rule you instead, Mademoiselle la Présidente."

"But of course!" Marie-Pier grinned back.

Mackenzie looked out over the quiet snowscape, the trees black and bare, the snow white and luminescent, the horizon a little too near, the stars hidden behind mirrored glâce, the quiet hum of machinery rippling the still and silent night. Inside the riblike maples, she could almost feel the sap forming, these trees somehow so much *fuller*, so much more *real*, than the American red maples outside, even stripped of their leaves and covered in snow.

"It *is* beautiful ..." she breathed. "I can't imagine what it looks like when it's falling."

"Yes," Marie-Pier sighed, "but where are the snows of yesteryear, no?"

Mackenzie's brow furrowed.

"Actually, yeah," she said, her mouth firing staccato English while her brain worked, "why *is* it so much hotter here on Lake St. Jean than down on the Saint Lawrence? Even given the stabilizing influence of the seaway and relative elevation and, y'know, other stuff, it *still* seems way too hot for the latitude and climate."

"I'm sure one of Dad's grad students has written a paper on it." Marie-Pier groused. "It's probably locked up in his collected lab notes somewhere."

"Think you could get it for me? Just to scratch the intellectual itch."

"He'll consider you an English *bosse de bêcosse* who thinks she knows Québec better than a pure-wool," Marie-Pier noted.

"Hey, I *know* what that means! Besides, if anyone is boss of the back-house, it's *him*. King of his little country of winter, his, how do you say, few acres of snow. It's only a paper, he won't mind."

"Careful. Kings tend to get upset in the face of truth." Marie-Pier sighed. "You aren't going to stop, are you? Fine. I'll get you a data key, on one condition."

"Yes?"

"You're not cooping yourself up with ecological data and a terminal all day. You and I will do skiing!"

Mackenzie's laugh broke any stillness left under the glass. It actually disturbed some snowpack off the nearest maple branch.

"*D'accord*," she squeaked between embarrassed fingers.

"Mec! Dépêchez! Allons-y! *Last one on her skis is a rotten egg!*"

"Wait!" Mackenzie replied. "You only got me this data key last night and your father's intranet is diabolic! My terminal's still compiling the granulated heat-map!"

"Then let it compile while we generate some heat, *dammit*!" Marie-Pier called, cursing in the English fashion. "Just get out here!"

Something about the heatmap seemed *wrong*, but Mackenzie couldn't put her finger on it. Obviously, this was a *real* 3D time-lapse climate model, not one of the worked-up examples in her textbook. Still, as Mackenzie reached out and rotated it in her hands, there *was* something … off. She cursed the sluggish intranetwork, and left it to compile before Marie-Pier got angry enough to become polite.

The model still hovered before her eyes, inscribed on her kerosene breaths as they huffed cross-country on their skis.

"Enjoyable, no?" Marie-Pier's voice was muffled behind the thick arrow-patterned scarf.

"You …" Mackenzie gasped, "… do this… for *pleasure?*"

Her side burned in defiance of the freezing-dry cold as she took another step.

"But of course!" Marie-Pier. "Half the pleasure is the cross-country. The other half is drinking hot coffee and hot soup and some Crown Royal at the other end."

"I think … I like … that half … better!"

"Don't worry, my summer-child. We're almost at the rivulet. We'll do a picnic there."

When they *did* arrive, seemingly a lifetime later, Mackenzie's heart hammered in her chest and she could not shuck her hood and toque and scarf fast enough. As the sweat froze on her overheated brow, Mackenzie had to admit that the sharp cold winter air almost felt … kind of nice. Detaching her ungainly skis definitely helped.

The rivulet, a tributary on the Péribonka that emptied into Lake St. Jean, was a long thin snake of dirty ice winding through the soft mounds of snow.

"You know, for all your Dad talked it up, I thought it would be bigger."

Mackenzie sniffed, and put on her best impression of Dr. Corriveau's regal tone. "Yes, Point-Taillon is ze only glâcehouse in Kebek who have ze riverrr inside, a whole *écologie* above and below ze waterrr!"

Marie-Pier laughed like tinkling bells in the frozen air.

"*Arrêtez!* Your French *joual* is terrible!" she said. "And in fairness to my father, not just Québec, but the whole *world*."

"But it's so dark and ugly!"

"Ah, that's just dirty rotten ice." Marie-Pier twirled the Thermos cap off with mittened fingers. "It sometimes gets like that. It is not easy to stop a river every winter."

"What do you mean?" Mackenzie asked, suddenly alert, her aching side and numbing nose forgotten. "When does it freeze?"

"In the summer, when we have all the panels open, it flows as free as air through the glâcehouse." Marie-Pier made a whooshing gesture. "But when she closes up at Thanksgiving, we have to freeze the water by hand with portable refrigerators. The waste-heat is awful; it always melts the snow on the banks so you get dirty mud. Good thing we came in December and no earlier."

Marie-Pier poured Mackenzie a Thermos cap of Crown Royal—fortified coffee, dark and bitter and, to Mackenzie's surprise, exactly what she needed. She drank it down absently, her mind whirling so hot she might have melted the snowbank by laying her head in it.

"Mec?" Marie-Pier said. "*Salut.*"

"*Oui, salut.*" She raised her cup and let it be clinked.

Her eyes were welded to the dirty ice of the rivulet, and the secrets frozen beneath it.

"Mec!" Marie-Pier sighed, striding into their shared cabin. "This has gone on for long enough. If you would please detach yourself from your terminal?"

Mackenzie looked up at her, with eyes that made the Princess of the History Department pause and take stock. In the days since their ski trip to the bank of the tributary, Mackenzie had massaged data until her fingers ached in the stuffy swelter of the cabin. As she eliminated extraneous factors with the plodding methodology of a nervous undergrad, the image came clearer and clearer. It looked like a black hole.

The 3D image hanging in the cabin meant nothing to Marie-Pier, for all her scholarly acumen in teasing out the causes leading to Québec's independence or the sharp eye with which she could compare manuscripts.

"I ... think I know." Mackenzie stuttered. "I think I know why Lac St.-Jean is so much warmer than Montréal. So much warmer than it should be."

"Yes, carbon emissions and greenhouse gasses." Marie-Pier snapped. "We do discuss climate change in the History department, Mec."

Mackenzie shook her head. "There's something I need to show you. You and your father."

"What, locked up in some room debating data points?"

"No, we need to go to the rivulet."

Marie-Pier's face changed. "You are serious."

Mackenzie nodded. "If I'm right, your father should know. And I need you to translate."

"Me? My specialty is politics, not ecological engineering."

"Don't you always say politics is the art of translating correctly?" Mackenzie said. "And that the Canadian confederation fell apart from lack of translating?"

Marie-Pier screwed her mouth shut, narrowed her eyes at Mackenzie... and nodded politely, turning on one heel and marching stiffly away.

Mackenzie gulped.

By the time she returned, with her father in tow, Mackenzie had already swaddled up for the march. This time, since day visitors were using all the skis, they wore snow shoes, or *raquettes*. The *raquettes* did not help her case.

"I hope that your blonde is better at scientific analysis than she is at snow-shoeing," Dr. Corriveau commented archly as Mackenzie took another lurch forward.

"She is a brunette." His daughter's reply was almost as dry as the frozen air.

"So how does your brunette intend to teach Québécois about winter?" Dr. Corriveau sneered. His French was textbook precise, to ensure Mackenzie understood. She understood perfectly well, the heat rising up her scarf-swaddled neck as they arrived at the rivulet. She wondered if her embarrassment was warm enough to melt its banks.

"I'll show you," Mackenzie huffed. "The climate model confused me, at first. Textbook models are much, much simpler. But even I could see that Lake St. Jean is too warm, and the waters of the Sanguenay also."

Marie-Pier's rapidfire translating was thick as a slice of Sanguenay *tourtière*, chock with just as much local flavor.

"But yes, from climate change." Dr. Corriveau spat. "Summer moving north."

"I tried to take into account as many variables as possible: global temperature rise, lowering albedo of the hills as the ice melted, basin effects from gasoline emissions..."

Dr. Corriveau listened intently as his daughter enumerated all the variables that Mackenzie had accounted for, and even gave a short, sharp nod of approval alongside the Gallic grunt. She pressed on, citing his seminal work and papers of her McGill professors as if she were narrating her thesis, until finally, both father and daughter said:

"Get to the point!" Marie-Pier at least added "if you please."

Mackenzie gulped.

"Ours is a problem of thermodynamics. The heat must go somewhere, *n'est-ce pas?* At other glâcehouses, it reflects into the air. The problem here in Point-Taillon is that not only does the heat reflect from the glâce into the surrounding air, but also *into the water*. The dark lake water laps up all the radiating heat the porcelain-white glâcehouse has to give, and retains it far better than the air does. *That* would explain the heat around the lake, so much worse than anywhere else in Quebec."

Marie-Pier's running translation sputtered to a stop and croaked in her throat. Her jaw hung for a moment as she stared with new eyes at her Albertan friend.

"... are you sure?" she asked, in stunned English.

"Yeah." Mackenzie nodded. "I am. Tell him?"

"*C'est pas necessaire.*" Dr. Corriveau waved it away, his cheeks blotched with anger. "I know well when I am insulted. You have an undergraduate who speaks like a slow six-year-old trying to teach me the trade I have spent thirty years of my life perfecting! I come to *preserve* winter, not destroy it. It is not because of me that Lac St.-Jean does not freeze in winter. It is because of the toxic, choking outflows of a sick civilization!"

His massive fists were clenching and unclenching, looking big and powerful enough to rip the branches off the sugar maples. Marie-Pier subtly slid from her father's side and close to Mackenzie.

"My father ..."

"*Et pis toé, ma 'tite fille, keske tu fais? T'es 'vek l'été.* The English, the Americans, the heat, the beetles, the cardinals, the damned mustards and jessamines, they are all of one skin!" Corriveau roared, in English. "*De nous sont les érables, les églises, l'hiver!*"

"My father told me when I was a girl that facts do not lie," Marie-Pier said, her voice as even and icy as her father's was overheated. Her perfect, international French had slid back into place. "Is there a way to check the facts?"

"But of course not!" Dr. Corriveau snapped. "It's only your blonde's wild fancy!"

"There is," Mackenzie said, her own cheeks burning with rage. "It's why I brought us all here. Under this very thin rotten ice is running water, *warm* water, carrying away all the waste heat of the glâcehouse."

"What ridiculousness!" Dr. Corriveau barked. "I assure you I do not hire fools. My own assistant cores the water-ice every—"

"And if your theory proves true, what is to be done?" Marie-Pier asked, ever the political animal.

Mackenzie took a deep breath.

"You'd have to open the glâcehouse," she said. "Like in summer. Allow the heat to exchange and a new equilibrium to form."

"Let summer flood in, is that it, English?" demanded Dr. Corriveau. His face burned like the summer sun. "Open the panels and let the last precious few sugar maples choke on the fetid air that you people bring with you, and wither, and die? No. Under the glâce, the snows of yesteryear are *safe*. I have closed the locks and polarized the light against summer's creeping encroachments. But yes, even to the frozen bed of the river! Voilà, English blonde!"

Dr. Corriveau shoved between the women, knocking Mackenzie aside as if he didn't deign to notice her. Only Marie-Pier's quick hands kept Mackenzie from tumbling into the snowbank, ass-first and *raquettes* up. With regal majesty and bitter ridicule in every gesture, the huge man stooped at the bank and unlatched his snow shoes. With deliberate, regal step, he marched onto the dark ice, each boot print resounding in the still air. For a moment, he stood, before turning and staring at both of them with dark, disdainful, burning eyes.

"The winter ice is solid all the way through." Each French word was a sharp, precisely-thrown dart. He even tapped the ice with his bootheel, just to nail the point home.

The heel plunged through on the fourth tap. Off-balance, the big man let out a startled cry and listed to one side, his other boot skidding out across the slick ice. The impact of his knee shattered more of the ice, and he slipped under the running waters of the rivulet.

Marie-Pier was first to react.

"*AU SECOURS!*" she cried. "Man in the water! Mec, help me get him out!"

Dr. Corriveau had risen partway from the water, as far as his knees, but his waterlogged mittens gave him no purchase on the slick ice and the surprising strength of the flowing waters beneath their mask of ice threw his feet out from underneath him.

Both Mackenzie and Marie-Pier scrambled the few feet to the bank, before Marie-Pier stabbed an arm out to stop Mackenzie's forward momentum. They took ginger paces, always testing the next step to see if the ice would hold each woman's weight over wide *raquettes*. The stinging cold of the water stabbed straight through Mackenzie's pant-leg as Dr. Corriveau splashed for purchase.

"*Voici*, under his armpit!" Marie-Pier spat.

"Sorry?" Mackenzie blinked. Marie-Pier wrapped her arms around her father's left shoulder. Mackenzie got the idea, grabbing the doctor around his right shoulder, heaving ineffectively.

"*Un, deux, trois!*"

The ice-sheet splintered a little more as they yanked the great bulk of Dr. Corriveau's back against it.

"*Un, deux, trois!*"

Mackenzie felt cracking under her left foot, and almost stumbled as she jumped back, her arms still firm around the doctor's body.

"*Un, deux, trois!*"

Now she felt a hundred hands on her own back, dragging her back to the firm hoarfrost and the doctor out of the water with her. The doctor's colleagues had come running from everywhere, and whirled like a winter cyclone to help their incoherent, spasming, soaking-wet professor.

The only coherent French that Dr. Corriveau could manage in the face of the flurry of questions and cries were: "Her! Get her out of here!" There were some choice Anglo-Saxon words thrown in, seemingly at random.

Marie-Pier looked up over her father's shoulder, from where she crouched and tried to rub warmth into his broad and bloodied back.

"*Merci beaucoup.*" She added, in English, "You'd better go. We'll meet up later."

Mackenzie thought fast, turning toward the little cluster of cabins and the lock. "Where you saw my face. Midnight."

Marie-Pier nodded, though her eyes were back on her shivering father. Mackenzie marched awkwardly back toward the exit, her shin aching with the sharp, wet cold.

She walked back to the glâcehouse for her midnight assignation, her every pore opened to the endless summer. Just a few days under the glâce, and the whole world felt new to her. She marched down to the lake shore, below the wall, and felt the chilly black water. It seemed impossible to her that it had once frozen under this same winter moon. The air around her was moist and muggy, even at midnight, chilly to her blood but still pregnant with ecosystem-wrecking power. Power that reflected off the white panels and fed the dark water.

In hindsight, it was obvious. Her eco-analysis professor, quoting Dr. Corriveau, said that all good science was.

The glâcehouse loomed over her, the imperious French staring down on her like one of Orwell's eyes as she crossed the Georgia mustards and Virginia-born jessamine. The glâcehouse was, among so many other things, an engineering marvel, the stuff of Buckminster Fuller's dreams. The materials science was beyond her ken, but she knew the gist. Impossibly thin and strong and light, and therefore, with human ambition, impossibly huge. It would take her a while to find the panel she'd been admiring when Marie-Pier had snapped at her, on that first night.

She knew it when she saw it. There, in the blank white polarized panels, there was a single triangle of darkness, at just about face height. Instead of her own pale face, though, Mackenzie saw there the drawn dark features of Marie-Pier Corriveau.

Marie-Pier's tired, relieved smile disappeared in a cloud of steaming breath. Into the cloud, she wrote with her finger.

"No sound."

From her bag, Mackenzie drew a tablet, writing on it with her own finger and holding it up.

"I came prepared."

Marie-Pier raised her eyebrows and nodded with approval. Mackenzie scribbled more.

"How's your dad?"

More breath, each letter appearing out of the fog.

"Better. Glad I stayed. Sorry."

"It's okay." Mackenzie scribbled. "Grabbed your car keys. Staying at the *auberge*."

Marie-Pier gave her a thumbs-up, then blew a blank palimpsest onto the glâce.

"You're right." Another breath. "About the heat." And another. This would take a while. "It's wrong: heating the whole Sanguenay for a few acres of snow."

Marie-Pier had lapsed into French, specifically Voltaire's dismissive phrase for all the Canadas. Mackenzie scribbled on her tablet.

"We have to open it up."

Marie-Pier nodded. She seemed relieved to not have to breathe so hard and make herself dizzy. Mackenzie cleared her screen, and scribbled again.

"Do you have any ideas how?"

"Papa's passwords—only way." breathed Marie-Pier. Then she drew a giant eye that stared at the words "*Mots de passe de Papa*." Mackenzie nodded, she understood: *It would draw attention.*

"Is there some other way?" she wrote.

In response, Marie-Pier illustrated two stick-figure girls tossing stones through a geodesic dome.

"That's horrible! I won't destroy a glâcehouse!" Mackenzie wrote. She thought for a moment. "Depolarize each panel, like you did with this one?"

"1000s of panels," Marie-Pier traced. "Takes forever."

"Plus we'd get caught." Mackenzie held up her screen. Marie-Pier nodded. "Isn't there a bypass to your Dad's passwords?"

"But of course," Marie-Pier mouthed. Then she drew a key around a neck. Her father's neck, of course.

Mackenzie had cleared her screen to reply when a funny look came over Marie-Pier's features. She stared intently at her finger drawing, the fog of breath already evaporating at the edges. Marie-Pier's sharp eyes fixed on the key.

Under it, she wrote a simple instruction: "Get the car. Ready to run."

"What will you do?" Mackenzie scribbled, holding it up with furrowed brow.

Without changing expression, Marie-Pier blew on the glâce one last time, tracing two words with her finger.

"Voilà Dahut."

As her breath faded, she was already gone.

Marie-Pier crept through the darkened silence of the house her father built, with its high shards of mirror for roof and walls, breaking the stillness only with misty breath and the soft, powdery crunch of snow under her boots. She kept quiet. Marie-Pier would have a devil of a time explaining herself to anyone if they heard her skulking around.

Devil of a time. Quelle drôle.

The dark timbers of the little clinic emerged from the dark hulks of the cabins. Inside, her father was wrapped in a dozen Hudson's Bay blankets and perched by the Roi du Soleil heating wire. It might have been overkill, but hypothermia was no joke. The old idiot! Marie-Pier didn't completely understand the science her father and Mackenzie had hurled at one another, but she'd taken enough rhetoric to know a poor argument when she heard it. She'd heard it in her father's thundering French, but not in the meek English of the tiny pale Albertan sweating under her toque.

And she'd read enough history to know that the *beau geste*, direct action for justice's sake, could be the start of something great. Hadn't Georgéline Legaré started out defending Montréal's Chinatown in the Allophone Riots of '33? And she'd become the first Présidente of the Republic. Restoring winter to the *pays d'hiver*, even one petty corner, surely counted as a *beau geste*. And no one on the green Earth could do it, except Marie-Pier Corriveau.

Because Marie-Pier Corriveau *remembered*.

She just hoped Mackenzie would have the Prius ready when Marie-Pier opened the locks. Direct action for justice usually required a fast getaway, unless you felt like becoming a martyr.

Marie-Pier knew the clinic door well enough to slip through with only the slightest click of the bolt. The tiny clinic was sweltering, almost as warm as Péribonka outside. The heat was oppressive; to use one of her father's favorite curses, it was *fetid*.

"My girl..." he rumbled. Marie-Pier nearly jumped from her skin, only keeping calm from a lifetime of being a black woman among whites.

"Papa," she breathed, "I ... brought you a drop."

He smiled to her.

"Alcohol is counter-indicated," he noted. "Dr. Tremblay would not approve."

"But also tradition, isn't it?" Marie-Pier frantically looked around the tiny clinic. There had to be a bottle of whisky stowed somewhere. "The ways of winter. Spirits to warm the frigid flesh."

"You have reason, my girl," he said.

There, in the tiny pharmacy. But of course old Gagnon would still be mixing medicines for his Professeur, and where Gagnon goes, so goes a fiddle and a bottle of Couronne Royale. While her father watched, she deftly unlocked the darkened pharmacy cabinet and snatched up the whisky.

"Share a drop with me?" he asked softly. "Like old times."

"Old times were you, me, and Maman." Marie-Pier noted, sitting in the empty chair.

"You have reason," he admitted. "How is she?"

"She is ... well. She moved back to Gatineau."

Dr. Corriveau made a face. "I don't understand why Canada doesn't just annex Gatineau and finish the job."

"Men like you would never allow it." Marie-Pier said, pouring a paper cup. "*Santé*, my father."

"*Santé*, my girl." They trinqued their paper cups, and slugged Gagnon's terrible-yet-patriotic whisky.

Marie-Pier had taken her first drop at the Reveillon when she was twelve, and her father had laughed as she coughed and sputtered. But now the tables were turned: she had grown up, and he had grown old. The paper cup slipped from his fingers after only two shots.

Marie-Pier laid her brown hand against the too-pink flush of her father's collarbone, began to carefully work the top few buttons. The data key with her name on it was just above his heart. He stank of chill sweats, exhaustion, and cheap whisky.

"Forgive me, father ..." she said, reaching in and wrapping her hand around the key.

A few moments later, the door clicked quietly shut again.

At first, she tried opening the MARIE-PIER system from the terminal in her cabin, but it was bounded on all sides by her father's high-security measures. As she'd crept toward the operations cabin, she saw shadows in the window: an overnight shift, monitoring the building in case someone like her should arrive to do exactly as she planned to do.

But there was another terminal, she knew, one basic and high-level enough to give the command she needed, unquestioned. It was mounted just above the inner lock, an emergency terminal in case of wildfire inside the glâcehouse.

Marie-Pier knew, because she had been the one to scrabble up and click it through when fire ate the old *cabane à sucre*. She was a little larger now than when she was thirteen, but she could still climb up. She remembered.

She shivered, and not from the frost of the metal burning through three layers of pant-leg. She knew Mackenzie's science was right, her father's wrong.

She knew she was the only one who could do the *beau geste* and open the locks to let winter free. She only resented the reasonable way the steps had all led up here, on top of the inner lock, digging with stinging fingers through the drift, excavating the built-in insulated terminal screen like some precious treasure.

It glowed like the winter sun, bright and cold. She waved the key before it, and watched the screen shift to the white and blue that bore her name. A few swiftly muttered commands, and the screen illuminated with three simple words: MODE D'ÉTÉ, ENGAGER?

"Ouais," she intoned.

The glâcehouse reflected red alarms, the still night shattered by ringing klaxons. Marie-Pier heard the creaking of icy metal on all sides as the *carrefour-rotors* groaned to life.

A slight wind blew the loose black wires of hair outside her cap. Marie-Pier found it within herself to blaspheme, before the second burst of wind blew her clear of the glâcehouse, out toward the lake.

The wind boomed hard enough to rock the Prius on its suspension, shocking Mackenzie from nervously refreshing the news. She looked up, across the little bridge to where the glâcehouse should be, and saw only a swirling dark miasma. Mackenzie watched it all unfold, even as something distantly splashed in the dark water.

Ecological engineering was all about systems thinking. "Always consider the whole," as her professors said. It was what Dr. Corriveau had failed to do when he raised a glâcehouse over running water. It was what Mackenzie failed to do when she suggested the glâcehouse be opened to the endless December summer.

A sudden rush of frozen air, enough to form its own internal weather system, into the warm, wet air of Lake St. Jean would cause precipitation. Clouds would form over the lake. And those clouds, pregnant with moisture, would burst.

Mackenzie smiled. She'd done it! Marie-Pier had done it! Somehow, she'd opened up the glâcehouse! And now Mackenzie understood why she'd asked her to have the Prius running. But where was she?

The minutes ticked by; searchlights and flashlights danced from within the unsealed glâcehouse and spread in a panicked scramble. Still no Marie-Pier. Mackenzie gulped with a too-dry throat. She tried to ring her over the network. Silence. Still no Marie-Pier.

The passenger door flew open. Mackenzie blinked away her phone screen.

It was a Corriveau, certainly. A very large, very pale Corriveau trembling with rage and with ... something else.

"Drive." he commanded. "For the dock."

Mackenzie drove, for the dock on the far side of Péribonka.

"I know that you put her up to it, English." he growled, adding a few extra Anglo-Saxon words. "You were her tempter."

"I don't even know what she did." Mackenzie's hands rattled on the wheel. "She told me to get the car ready and wait. She was going to do something big, but she didn't tell me what or how."

"The *beau geste*." rumbled Dr. Corriveau. He stank of cheap whisky. "She stole my data key and climbed up the enviro-lock and activated the firesafe protocol. If I'd been up and able, she never would have had a chance, not even my girl, but those—"

The French finally processed through Mackenzie's brain.

"On top of the lock?" her voice rose. "When the glâcehouse opened? Oh my God, she must have been straight in the wind!"

"I could have told you that, you little English blockhead!" Dr. Corriveau barked. His glâcehouse was one thing, but he became truly *fearsome* when it was Marie-Pier. "You arrogant little blonde! You are only fortunate she was thrown clear of the plaza and the rocks."

"Into the lake?"

He nodded. "We will do a boat, and search. She's been in the water ten minutes, and the temperature is dropping."

"I know where she is." Mackenzie's voice was preternaturally calm, even to her. "I'm turning around."

Dr. Corriveau's grip slapped on her wrist like a manacle. She instinctively pulled to a stop by the roadside.

"You don't know a goddamn. Now drive. Straight for the dock, English."

"Doctor Corriveau, I knew a goddamn about the heat in the water, I knew a goddamn that the cold is coming before you did, and I know a goddamn where Marie-Pier is. I saw the splash. I didn't know what goddamn it is before. Now I know goddamn that she dies if we are too long!" Mackenzie spluttered between French and English to get her point across.

For a long time, Corriveau just peered at her with narrowed eyes, like she was an unexpected serpent in his garden, and he was trying to discern if she was a helpful garter snake or a poisonous rattler. He looked up and out toward the glâcehouse, through the frosting windshield. The air grew colder, even through the glass.

"Where was the splash?" he croaked.

Mackenzie pointed. Not far from shore.

"Turn around. Over the Péribonka bridge," he said. "I will have them drop the barricades. Do your lights toward the waters."

Mackenzie already had the Prius in motion, rocketing back toward the glâcehouse. The car barricades slid to the planks as she clicked the high-beams on. The tires kicked up cobbles and wet-winter species like Georgia mustards and jessamine. Mackenzie eased the Prius forward toward the lake as far as she dared, the car's high beams lifting the dark waters to a muddled grey.

There was no Marie-Pier there.

The frosty air as they disembarked the car struck Mackenzie by surprise.

"It'll snow," she burbled. She ignored the worst Gross Eyes she had ever seen on a Québécois, peering at the lapping water. *"Comment dit-on* tide?"

Enlightenment dawned on the great man's brow, and he looked down toward the narrow strip of sand at the water's edge. He gave a howl and moved as if he would step down to the beach, to the freezing water, until Mackenzie thrust an arm out.

"But no." Mackenzie's French had a steel in it that rang like Marie-Pier's. "You are, er, hyperthermic. Let me do."

Before the old man could object, Mackenzie was already down to the shore and knee-deep in Lac St.-Jean, the ice swirling around her thighs. New and colorful curses burst in her head, and she hoped the *en colère* could keep a body warm. She heard what she assumed were new and colorful French curses behind her.

From down here, it was easy to see why he howled. A little ways from the shore, a stone spire thrust from the lake. Around this spire, a tangle of limbs batted limply at the rock in the darkness.

Mackenzie pressed forward, despite the protests of her shocked limbs at any kind of concerted effort in favor of shivering and spasming at the unbridled cold. The shore gave way gently, but Mackenzie's frigid, waterlogged feet found less and less purchase as she approached the spire. With a last burst of angry heat, she thrust forward and clutched one of Marie-Pier's dark limbs. Her heart fell. In her numbing hands, Marie-Pier's arm was not much warmer than the icy slurry they drifted in.

Mackenzie wrapped her arms around her friend, the blood rushing into her arms as she held fast, her legs kicking and spasming back toward the lapping lake shore. At last, huge hands gripped her and hauled her forward, out of the water. Her body was so benumbed and so confused that the change in temperature didn't even register on her consciousness. Someone else wrapped a blanket around her, and someone else waved a steaming cup of something in front of her. It smelled like hot chocolate. She drank.

Next to her were distant cries as they stripped Marie-Pier, and swaddled her in her own warm blanket, and Dr. Corriveau pleaded in sing-song French for his daughter to come back, to come home.

Something landed on Mackenzie's nose. Dr. Corriveau let out an unmistakable cry of joy. Then Mackenzie heard the most wonderful sound.

"Look, Papa, snow . . ." Marie-Pier's eyes were bloodshot. She caught Mackenzie's gaze and gave her a wan smile. *"Voilà,* the snows of yesteryear."

Contributors

James Howard Kunstler (cover art) is the author of twenty books and blogs at www.kunstler.com.

WB Rice works as a geologist for a California state water resource agency and lives with his family on the fringes of the LA–Orange County megalopolis. He likes to read fiction and non-fiction that challenges his mind. He appreciates the many aspects of nature and wonders what it might be like to live here on Turtle Island in the future. He particularly likes the solace and silence of the western desert and hopes to return sometime in the future as a proto- or neo-fremen. He is intrigued by ruins and inspired by the Shelley poem *Ozymandias*.

Justin Patrick Moore's radio work first appeared on the airwaves of Anti-Watt, a pirate station run on the campus of Antioch College. After dropping out of college he got a job and met the folks who got him onto WAIF where he became a co-host and programmer for the shows *Art Damage* and *On the Way to the Peak of Normal*, the latter of which he took over for several years after its founder retired from the air. He gave the show up to focus on writing, but found radio was hard habit to quit, and became a ham, KE8COY. Friendships forged in the shortwave community have led him to regularly contribute segments for the shortwave programs *Free Radio Skybird* and *Imaginary Stations*. He still fills in on occasion at WAIF for the underground music program *Trash Flow Radio*.

Clint Spivey spent several years working in meteorology for the US government in Europe and Asia. Launching balloons was always one of the more pleasant parts of the job. The recent supply chain failures around the world got him thinking of weather forecasting and how the field might be effected in the future. Unfortunately, he never participated in any rocketsondes.

Wesley Stine was born in Arizona, to parents from Indiana, and he currently lives in Georgia, where he is working toward a doctorate in physics at Emory University. His studies there have included a lot of work on molecular biophysics, as well as a project where he trained a simple AI to analyse the postures of rats. As a small child, Wesley was fascinated by cats, and also by mechanical clocks, and he would often spend hours making fanciful drawings of them. So when ChatGPT came out last December, it was only natural that one of the first things he asked it to do was to write a short story about a kitten who tries to catch the bird inside a cuckoo clock.

Cal Bannerman is a freelance copywriter, editor and audiobook producer from Scotland. Their writing is published in *Extra Teeth*, *Gutter*, *The Interpreter's House*, and *Reflex Fiction*. They were longlisted for the Cymera–Shoreline of Infinity Prize for Speculative Short Fiction 2023, and served as Marchmont Makers Foundation's inaugural writer-in-residence in June 2023. "Lights Out" forms part of a larger work-in-progress, tracing the gradual collapse of humanity through poetry, flash, prose and script, all set in the poster child of modern metropolises: Tokyo, Japan.

Anthony St. George lives with his husband in the San Francisco Bay Area where daily urban and rural hikes, as well as remnants of his Ph.D. in Classical Chinese and Korean Literature, inspire his stories. He has been published in a variety of publications, most recently *The Ocotillo Review*, *ChromeBaby*, and *New Maps*. Links to his published stories and artwork at: https://anthonystgeorge.com/.

R. Jean Mathieu has hauled sail, hung beef, organized unions, and joined the SFWA. His work can be found at www.rjeanmathieu.com.

Comments for contributors sent to the editor will be forwarded.

COLOPHON

New Maps is typeset by the editor using an ancient, temperamental program called LaTeX which nevertheless produces unsurpassable results. The text font is an early digital version of Hermann Zapf's Palatino—resurrected from abandoned files and fitted with modern amenities like kerning tables—which retains all the calligraphic warmth of the 1950s original cut that was lost in the production of the popular Linotype version. Titles are set in Sebastian Nagel's 2010 typeface Tierra Nueva, which is based on lettering from a 1562 map of the Americas; headers, drop caps, and miscellany are in Warren Chappell's classic Lydian; monospace text uses Spline Mono.

ACKNOWLEDGMENTS

Thanks this time go to all the usual suspects who help me maintain sanity while trying to juggle too many balls, and to all readers for their patience with delays in correspondence and sending of magazines that have been longer than they should during this chaotic summer. Thank you all.

Printed in Great Britain
by Amazon